A Bleu Streak

Summer

T.I. LOWE

ISBN: 1534872825
ISBN-13: 978-1534872820

DEDICATION

Happy 10th Birthday Lydia Lulu Lowe.
I love you to the moon and back!

ALSO BY T.I. LOWE

Lulu's Café
Goodbyes and Second Chances
A Bleu Streak Christmas
The Reversal
Coming Home Again
Julia's Journey
A Discovery of Hope
Orange Blossom Café

ACKNOWLEDGMENTS

A special thank you to my fabulous readers for appreciating my imperfect Bleu Family. You get what I'm trying to do with them and that just makes my day!

Thank you to Renee Kinlaw, author of God Has a Scrub Brush. This book helped me to wrap my heart and mind around past hurt and how important it is to forgive it and let it go. Still struggling as Max did, but I'll get there.

Thank you to Bernie and Nate for suggesting we send Will on a wild goose chase for his initiation. Sorry, but I couldn't let him get away with having to do it buck-naked.

Lydia, thank you for always being present and encouraging your momma!

My beta readers, Sally Anderson, Trina Cooke, Lynn Edge, and Jennifer Strickland. You girls help me keep the story on track. Y'all rock!

To Jan Carol, my editing lady! Thanks for cleaning up my sloppy typos and for guiding a sentence into making better sense.

Lastly, but always firstly, my Heavenly Father. You are a good, good father. Thank you for loving me and accepting my flaws. And also for allowing me the epic opportunity of sharing your incredible love with the world.

Abandoned

"I Will Buy You a New Life"
-Everclear

Abandoned… What a perplexing word. First meaning of this word is deserted, left unattended, having to fend for one's self. I get it. But then it also means to be reckless, unrestrained, uninhibited. I get that as well. My life has seen me living both sides of the confusing word—first meaning from no choice of my own, but the second I claim all responsibility.

One early morning, I claimed my freedom. With my five string—yes, one was missing—Fender strapped to my back with an old leather belt serving as a makeshift strap and a duffle bag filled with my hand-me-down wardrobe, I walked away from my childhood before the sun could rise and catch me. Loaded up in a beat-up van with my boys, all five of us teenagers thought we knew everything and had it all figured out. As I sat on a hard floor in the back of that van, my eyes focused on the rusted side door instead of the grimy back window, swearing to never look back.

Youthful, dumb, and just naïve enough to think I could leave that abandoned kid behind. Poor kid was starved for more than just food.

Now in my advanced thirties, still dumb and naïve enough to think I can keep running from him. Maybe the age—how did I get so blame old—is starting to slow me down enough to allow things to begin catching up with me. That scrawny kid is still starving, but he has gotten faster than me.

My old Fender, with grooves worn into the finish along the neck from my fingertips, rests behind a glass case nowadays as a reminder of where this crazy-cool life was launched—a shed behind the trailer park, no less. My first guitar and the hundreds of others I've collected over the years are a testament to all the struggles my music family has overcome. But that success didn't help us overcome everything.

You can't buy a new life if you're shackled to a deep hurt the past carelessly inflicted. Cars, houses, and other shiny new possessions will all fade to rust and will have to be replaced eventually. But you only get one life, no matter how fat the bank account, so somehow it's up to us to figure it out.

I have failed at figuring it out.

My friend, who is more of a sister figure, says we have no choice where we come from, but we can choose where we go. Jewels used to have a hang-up with the white-trash stigma she inherited from her childhood. She always felt insignificant simply because stupid people looked down on her for living in a tin-can trailer and wearing secondhand clothes. Jewels is farthest from insignificant, and people, like the ones on the opposite side of the lake haven't a clue in their pampered, thick skulls as to how amazing she is. The chick is pure and that heart of hers is the richest I've ever witnessed. Her nickname suits her better than any of ours. Jillian will always be our Jewel. She's sacrificed more than any of us for our betterment.

Dillon is Dimples. Dude got a pair that makes the girls swoon no matter what.

Mave is Klutz for obvious reasons. Ask

him how many bones he's broken, and he'll ask you how many does he got.

Logan is Mr. Mellow. The guy is smooth. I'm pretty sure he's unable to yell or get angry or say a word without adding a melody to it.

Trace is normally called Space Cadet. Dumb-blond jokes follow him around wherever he wanders off to, and he's earned every one of them.

I've gotten stuck with the nickname Pepper Man, thanks to my sister-in-law Izzy, aka Doll Baby. I might have brought that on myself, but pranks are part of my DNA. There's no denying them. I guess that's better than my old nickname. *Wormy*. With motivation from a personal trainer and a contract with this protein shake company, I've worked hard on ridding myself of that image. The company tried at one point to buy me out of the contract due to my frame stubbornly refusing to pack on any weight. Eventually we got enough muscle on me to run a campaign and call it done. I'm just naturally slim with a weird jacked-up metabolism. The girls of our group hate me a little for this.

So where was I before my thoughts got carried away…

Oh yeah. My issues… Don't we all have

them?

Growing up in a two bedroom trailer with sagging floors and having to make do with secondhand *everything* was never an issue for me like it was for Jewels and the others. Some may say it's because I didn't know any better.

Wrong.

The poverty struggle was real, but that was something I knew how to survive. Other matters, the ones that secretly bruise your soul, were where my struggle was deeply rooted. My plan of escape as a teen wasn't from the trailer park or poverty. Not even close. I was running away from my father abandoning me and my twin brother like we were debris left from his wrecked life—easily discarded and forgotten.

Turns out my plan was in vain, because the abandonment issue lingers like an unwieldy shadow, never allowing the sun permission to touch me. So I have to make my own sunshine by doing stupid stuff—my crowd calls it stupid, but I just call it having fun and blowing off some burdening steam.

Everyone says, "Grow up, Max!"

I say, "The heck with that! I ain't gotta! And I ain't gonna!"

Laughter feels better than the alternative.

Laughter keeps running off the dark sadness for at least a spell.

Laugher won't allow me to break… completely.

Laughter has never abandoned me for long.

ONE

"Peaches"
-The Presidents of the U.S. of America

The May afternoon lazily swept by with the Bleu family paying it no mind. In the midst of the Bleu Peach Orchard, an elaborate pergola allowed the Georgian sunshine to glance through its cedar planks and play along the large gathering as they celebrated life. The group had witnessed many blessings in the form of marriages, babies, and career successes, but that day was set aside to celebrate the first kid to join their family. Will Bleu had not only graduated from high school, but had also been awarded a full music scholarship for college. His parents had secured college funds years ago, so he humbly declined the scholarship and asked that it be awarded to someone with more of a financial need. It was an honor to have been awarded just the same to him and his family. Yes, a lot to be celebrated indeed.

Still proudly wearing his graduation cap proclaiming "He Willed it!" that glittered in the sun—thanks to Mave taking Grace's Bedazzler to the top of it—he set into opening the stack of gifts. He made quick work of tearing open a black envelope. Studying its contents, the young man's head jerked up with his dark-blue eyes lit in excitement.

"No way!" he yelled, waving the thick card embossed with intricate designs.

"Yes way!" Dillon exclaimed, matching Will's enthusiasm. "We all have it and now that you're eighteen and about to set out in your adult life, I think it's time."

Jen snorted as she handed Trace their blond toddler, who was anxiously reaching for his daddy. Casio was making a game of going from one lap to the other, and then back again. "Only because Jewels gave Dillon permission is why Will can finally get his first tattoo." The crowd laughed as she mocked Dillon, trying to mimic his deep voice, "*I* think it's time."

Max leaned over and studied the logo on the card for Case Art. "We get to make a trip to Charleston. Hot dang!" After cramming another forkful of cake into his mouth, he mumbled, "Mave, your Doll Baby might as well get hers while we're there."

Each member of their motley crew had the same tattoo on their hip, an unofficial family emblem. Ecclesiastes 4:9-10 was inked as a reminder that they would always have one another's backs and remain by their side through thick or thin. They had wisely figured out that life on your own can hand out a lot of downfalls, but with your brother or sister by your side as well as God, you tend to have less falls and can get back up easier when one occurs.

"Now that Mona has that fat diamond on her finger, she gonna get it, too?" Mave fired back, giving Max a look that no one else seemed to catch. Going on the defense on Izzy's behalf was second nature to the drummer, and he knew his wife was skittish about needles.

Cramming in another chunk of cake, Max shrugged and gave as honest of an answer as he could. "I don't know."

"Brooke has it," Logan's mellow voice

chimed in as he combed his fingers through his wife's honey-blonde hair as she sat on his lap. Her mocha skin seemed to sparkle in the rich sunrays as she gazed at her husband.

"Speaking of Mona. That's one busy woman. When are we going to see her again?" Jewels asked.

Max's shoulder hitched up before he could stop it. "Being a publicist keeps her slammed all the time. She should be able to make it to the Music Festival Awards next month."

"Good. We've got to catch up on the wedding planning," Izzy commented as her eyes wandered over to the children frolicking under the peach trees.

"I think them two are trying to get into the book of world records for the longest engagement in history," Trace joked, but Max showed no interest one way or the other.

"It's going to be a family reunion out in California. Kyle plans on staying at least two weeks. Right, Pretty Girl?" Dillon asked, glancing at Jewels.

"Yep. Leona and Phoebe will be there most of the summer. She's bringing her assistant Stella to help with the beach house remodel. I think it'll do her good to get away." Jewels voice went quiet. "I can't even imagine how it felt to lose her husband so suddenly. Grant was everything to her."

"It's hard to believe it's been almost two years since the car accident," Jen added in a quiet voice as well.

Silence overtook the large group for a bit, somber eyes set on the children at play while their thoughts were clearly with the young widow and her daughter.

Max broke the silence abruptly. "Mave, your kid has something crammed in his mouth."

"Ludwig!" Mave hollered as he hurried over and began fishing around his son's mouth with his un-casted hand, eventually pulling out not one but two peach pits.

The little guy pushed a brown curl off his face, sticking his tongue out and wrinkling his tiny nose. "It smell good. Taste nasty. Yuck!"

Mave chuckled while mussing the toddler's hair.

"That kid is just as curious as his dad and always looking for something to eat," Trace taunted, shaking his head. "And y'all messed him up with that name. There's other drum brands that ain't so weird. At least you did right by Pearl."

"You're one to talk, naming your two after

keyboard brands." Mave spun around to fix Trace with a glare, but lost his footing in the loose soil, nearly tripping headfirst into a tree.

"Dude!" Dillon yelled before releasing a gruff sigh in frustration. "Don't go breaking your other arm!"

The clumsy drummer threw both hands in the air, one sporting a black cast dressed in custom "cast tattoos" in a flame pattern that covered from his right elbow to the tip of his knuckles, as he shot Dillon that glare intended for Trace. "*Chill*, man. All's good!"

No sooner had the words gotten out of his mouth, than Trace's rambunctious four-year-old son Roland ran by whacking Mave in the eye with the stick he was waving around with considerable potency for such a little kid. Mave's hand flew up to protect the offensive spot, but with a little too much surprised force, adding a self-inflicted sting from the cast. He stumbled around while grumbles and moans murmured from him unintelligibly.

"Good grief! And that, ladies and gentlemen, is the Maverick King Train-Wreck Show!" Max applauded with the group joining in, the roar of laughter deafening.

"Trace, you and Jen have two wild boys," Izzy said affectionately.

"Ugh. Don't I know it? I'm so outnumbered." Jen turned her attention toward Mave. "Sorry about that."

"No worries." His glassy eyes blinked in a rapid twitching manner as though they were trying to rid the pain while holding back tears. "Jen, you wouldn't be outnumbered if you'd learn how to spit 'em out in pairs, one each, like me."

"Like you?" Izzy raised her dainty eyebrows.

"I did my part, Doll." Mave leaned over and kissed his wife's pouty lips before settling back down in his chair. "But your part was epic in comparison." He winked his good eye at her, eliciting a faint blush to color her cheeks.

Everyone went back to devouring the orange pineapple cake Izzy made at Will's request, but Dillon wasn't done with the broken arm discussion just yet.

"Still can't get over how you managed to break your arm playing golf, of all things," Dillon said with no amusement. He rubbed the dark scruff on his chin while frowning at the casted reminder that Mave would not be able to open the summer tour. Good thing another plan had been in place long before his friend's blunder off the side of a steep tee box.

"And I still can't believe anyone in their right mind would finish playing the tournament *with* a broken arm." Izzy shook her head.

"But we won didn't we?" Mave defended, finally breaking Dillon's glare. Both men shared proud grins and fist bumps. It was the first time they had won the coveted celebrity golf tournament.

"That does merit solid bragging rights," Max chimed in, knowing good and well his only contribution to that winning title was driving one of the golf carts. Several sets of female eyes shot in his direction, so he quickly added, "It was all for a great cause. Our charity got a chunk of change."

"I think Music Notes would have been just fine without prize money at the expense of Mave's safety," Jewels added while offering Casio another bite of cake while Jen was distracted with scowling at Max.

Will gave up waiting for them to hash out the delusion of keeping Mave safe—lost cause—and moved to the next gift. He opened a rectangle, revealing a leather checkbook along with information about his new account.

"Thanks, Momma. Did y'all put me a fat

deposit in it?" He waggled his thick eyebrows as black as his head full of hair while grinning widely. The young man was the spitting image of his father.

Chuckles rang out amongst the crowd as the breeze picked up, carrying the sweet aroma of peaches around with it. The season was close at hand, apparent with the trees beginning to slouch under the abundant weight of the ripening fruit.

"Nope. Just the amount needed to open the account," Jewels answered while slipping Jen's little guy another bite of her cake, but Jen caught her and shot a warning look at her. Casio had already eaten his and most of Jen's slice, but Jewels couldn't resist his plea for more.

"One hundred bucks?" he read from the paperwork before looking up in question in the direction of his parents.

"You gotta start earning your own cash, kid. Maybe a summer job can help fatten it up." Dillon added along with a wry grin he shared with his bandmates.

"Here, open mine. It's much cooler than that." Mave tossed Will a long box.

Will reverently pulled out a set of custom drumsticks from the case as a gasp escaped his stunned lips. "Dude… These are killer." The first thing he noticed was the Bleu Streak band logo embossed on the ends. Then his eyes zoned in on his very own signature engraved in the wood with a deep-blue hue coloring it in. He held the sticks high, showing them off to everyone.

Grace leaned close to inspect them. "Wow, those are so pretty."

Will cut his eyes to his younger sister. "Wrong word. So not pretty. They are bad with a capital *A*."

"Son!" Jewels scolded, then cut her eyes to Max.

"What?" he garbled out around a mouthful of cake, his third piece. "It's not saying the curse."

"You know good and darn well that still implies it," Jen piped in.

"And what does *darn* imply, Henny?" he asked, using her nickname. The guys had declared her the mother hen of them a long time ago, especially concerning the rowdy King twins. He swatted the fork in the air, dismissing her glare, before pointing to another box. "Dude, open mine next."

Will tore open the music themed wrapping paper and pried the lid off a small silver case.

"Guitar picks with the year and Bleu Streak Logo." The grin on Will's face said he loved them, but he couldn't help but poke fun at the group. "What? Did some logo company give y'all a discount for all this loot?"

"You'd think," Logan piped in as he tossed Will another gift box.

He pulled out a black T-shirt with the Bleu Streak logo on the front and Summer Tour Dates listed on the back—all the lettering was vibrant in electric blue and metallic silver. "Cool…" The young man's voice trailed off as his eyes landed on the gift tucked in the midst of the list of band member's names—Will Bleu. The hodgepodge of gifts finally made sense. "Dude!" He hopped up so fast the sparkly graduation cap flew off.

Dillon wrapped him in a manly hug with the rest of the band members circling around them. "You ready to become official? The pay's okay, but the hours can sometimes be lousy."

The guys roared in laughter. Will had played with them for years, but this was them finally announcing him as their bandmate to the world.

Will looked over his shoulder toward the twins. "Which one of you old farts is retiring?" This earned another round of unruly laughs and howls.

"We ain't that old," Mave answered for them both.

Will glanced at Trace and Logan. "I'm not the strongest on bass or the keys, but I guess I can hold up lead vocals." He gave his dad a sly look.

"I'm not old either, kid. You gonna rock out wherever we feel like putting you."

"I can handle that."

"Good, 'cause we need to get a summer tour in before you go off to college. That should fill your checking account up for a while. Then during winter break, we gotta get into the studio."

No way could they have ever given Will a better graduation gift than allowing him a summer of touring as an official bandmate of Bleu Streak. Music was not just part of his soul, but the very material it was fashioned from and he knew he was born to create and share it with the world. The young man knew he wouldn't have to do it on his own. The people surrounding him on that warm May day had built this dynamic family on a firm rock of faith and loyalty, and Will Bleu was honored to be a part of it.

TWO

"On My Own"
-Vincent Vincent and the Villains

"Day One" (Acoustic)
-Matthew West

Any house, no matter if it's a twelve-bedroom-three-story mansion, will become a cacophony of ruckus when over twenty head of people are gathered. Specifically the bunch residing in the Bleu's beach house for an entire summer. Before landing in California, the group drew for bedroom assignments. Max lucked up and drew the coveted bottom floor that would serve as his room, the gym, and the band's practice studio. And that was all fine by him. The solace of having an entire floor to himself at night was beyond appealing, especially with the funk he had found himself stuck in as of late.

"Hair-cutting time. Get the lead out!" Mave hollered halfway down the stairs before backtracking. It was the third time he had made the trek and irritation had accompanied him that time.

Max had been glued to the couch, staring at the unanswered text—*I miss you*—he sent Mona over two hours ago. Giving up, he pocketed the phone and tried to get in the spirit of the afternoons shenanigans. Dillon promised him, and so it was time to go make good on it. Max cracked his neck, excitement finally building for the opportunity to go blow off some steam, before pushing into his boots and heading upstairs.

The rest of the guys were already loaded up in the oversized black SUV by the time he managed to scarf down a snack of three PB&J sandwiches and a quart of milk. He climbed in and met a stony reception of impatient faces.

"You do realize we are on a tight schedule today, right?" Blake, the band's sometimes-annoying but mostly cool assistant, grumbled, his light golden-brown eyes somehow managing to hold an icy glare.

Max was leaning toward the annoying bit at the moment. He offered up a passive shrug. "We're the band. We *are* the schedule."

Trace snorted. "Even I know better than that."

The crowd released a low chuckle at the keyboardist cracking a joke at his own expense. Common sense sometimes confused the blond guy, but he had enough to accept his character flaw for what it was.

"I don't see why we had to wait on slowpoke for haircuts anyway. Dude ain't got any hair to cut." Will pointed to Max, who was sporting a military buzz.

Max rubbed his hand through his hair, measuring the top that finally felt to be at least a half inch long. "Still not over that stunt," he muttered.

The guys got ahold of him with a pair of clippers while Dillon and Logan sat on him a few months back. By the time Jen broke it up, the damage was done and poor Max resembled a dog with the mange. Shaving off the remaining chunks of chestnut hair was the only solution.

The guys kept ribbing him all the way to

the salon and Max kept ignoring them. He was an expert at dishing it out and had learned long ago how to take it as well. Besides, he had a pocket full of fun just waiting to be handed out.

Twenty minutes later, Will sat in the chair staring at the mohawk Max was allowed to carve into his thick black hair. One minute the stylist was whirling the chair away from the mirror to get started, and then the next the chair was whirled back around to reveal Max standing behind him, wearing a wide grin while holding a pair of clippers.

Will shrugged his shoulder, unperturbed, as he coasted his fingers through the spiky middle. "It's cool. I always wanted a mohawk, but Momma wouldn't let me."

The grin fell from Max's face as he cut his eyes to the other guys. "Some initiation."

Will bellowed in laughter. "This is the initiation. Man, you old geezers are slipping. Anyway, I thought the tattoo was for that."

"It was part of it…" Dillon said as he leaned closer with narrowed eyes and studied something behind his son's right ear. "But that weren't. Plus it's old ink." He knocked the boy upside his head with a bit of force. "What are you doing, hiding something from me?"

The other guys leaned around to see what the fuss was all about and saw for the first time a tattoo that had been kept hidden underneath Will's shaggy hair. An intertwining J and D were tucked behind his ear.

"Like father, like son," Mave said on a chuckle with the other guys joining in.

"It's my reminder to always listen to my righteous parents," Will added in a mocking tone, earning another whack to the head. He had to know it was coming with him poking fun at his dad proclaiming something similar about his own first tattoo that had been hidden in the exact same spot. Dillon's was a tribute to his late father.

"Well, it's done you no good, if you're doing junk behind my back." Dillon shook his head. "Not cool. Wait till your mom sees it."

That comment wiped the smirk off the little-too-cocky guy's face. "Dude!"

"Don't *dude* me." Dillon pulled out his wallet and paid generously for the salon allowing the prank and for the others' hair trimmings. "Let's roll out. Next stop is wardrobe."

"Wardrobe?" Trace whined, looking pained at the very idea, with the others grumbling their disapproval.

"Since when did you guys start putting up with junk like that?" Will glanced over the group, all clad in various loose-fitting well-worn jeans and dark tees with either Vans or Chucks or scuffed boots on their feet. "And what's wrong with what we're wearing now?"

All eyes darted over to Tate, one of their longtime managers. The redhead's hands shot up in defense. "Don't kill the messenger. Sometimes you have to do what the suits at the record label request on special occasions." He pointed toward the door, leading the group outside.

After they were loaded back up Will asked, "What's so special this time?"

"Summer concert kickoff performance headlining our newest, hottest member. Nuff said," Logan answered in his lazy drawl while sliding his aviator sunshades over his gold eyes.

"Yeah. The label is pulling out all the stops for *the* Will Bleu," Trace added, which provoked the desired effect on the young guy. Will looked right smug.

Max averted his face toward the window to conceal the grin as the others took to egging the cockiness right out of the young guy until the SUV pulled into the backlot of a private studio.

"Sonny, it won't take us long. You wanna wait here?" Dillon asked their bodyguard who was doubling as driver for the day.

"Sounds like a plan," the giant of a man agreed with a knowing look.

Dillon nodded his head and leaned over the seat to offer Sonny a fist bump before climbing out.

The group barely made it inside the side door before a team of stylists surrounded them. Each band member was given a garment bag and ushered to a dressing room. There was no denying the excitement in Will's grin as he spotted the nametag identifying the bag belonging to Will Bleu/Drummer.

"This way, handsome," a young woman, wearing oversized maroon glasses that practically shrouded her entire face, cooed as she escorted him to the middle dressing room. "Try the outfit on and then let us have a looksee on how it fits."

She pulled the thick curtain shut to allow him some privacy. Zippers being unzipped and rustling of fabric sounded from Will's dressing room, followed by several struggling grunts. Then...dead silence.

"What the heck... No way! We ain't

dressing like a flipping boyband!" he hollered in disgust and then added a growl for good measure.

"Language, kid," Dillon reprimanded.

"Momma said *ain't* is in the dictionary," he called out.

"You know what word I'm talking about." Dillon glanced over at the line of guys standing in front of Will's dressing room ready to pounce.

"It's ya'll's fault my son talks the way he does."

"What's wrong with the way he talks?" Max asked, shrugging that shoulder as always.

"What are you guys doing out there?" Will asked as suspicion slowly dripped into his inquiry.

"We're already dressed. Just waiting on you, *slowpoke*. Hurry it up. We're on a tight schedule," Max said sarcastically, getting his jab in for both smart remarks from earlier.

"I ain't wearing this cr—" The word froze on Will's tongue as he slung the curtain open. He was decked out in bright-white super-skinny jeans that were loudly paired with bulky, neon-pink high-tops and a purple tank top with Pretty Boy emblazed in metallic gold across the front.

Before the poor kid could react to the entire group still donning their earlier attire, all five guys ambushed him. Not going down without a fight, Will bucked and kicked and wiggled as his bandmates grabbed hold of him and carried him outside, leaving his personal clothes and most of his pride behind. As soon as they had him wrestled into the backseat, the guys loaded up and Sonny sped off before he could make a break for it. He glared at his dad on one side of him and then to Logan on the other, knowing the two biggest guys of the band had him trapped. All three sat shoulder to shoulder.

Will kept fidgeting in the pinching pants while eyeing the red-faced group. Heavy wheezing heaved out as their chests rose and fell in a labored pace.

"Why are you old geezers so winded?" Will asked, but no one seemed in the mood— or maybe due to the lack of breath—to reward his taunt with a response.

The silence held until everyone's breathing slowed back to normal.

"Mave, why's your lip bleeding?" Dillon asked, knowing Jen or one of the other women or probably all of them would surely wring them out for instigating another Mave booboo.

Mave cautiously dabbed at his lip. "You're six-three two-hundred-pound baby punched me while he was jack-rabbiting around like a fool."

Will leveled his mentor with a look. "I'd apologize if I was sorry, but I'm not." He held up his arm, showing off an angry whelp. "That dang cast of yours hurts."

"Language," Dillon growled, shaking his head.

The SUV pulled up to the undisclosed destination. Max looked out the window before pulling his own secrets out of his pocket. "You've got a good hour or so to find your way to the concert." He handed Will a list of concert venues.

"But in the meeting I remember Tate saying we're at Hollywood tonight," Will shot back, thinking he had one-upped them again.

"Did I say Hollywood?" Tate's grin was all the evidence needed to show he was in on the scheme, too.

"Sounds like you should have paid attention to that tour date shirt I gave you for graduation, bro." Logan's lips pulled into a lazy grin as he handed Will his wallet. "You best be on with it."

"What about my phone?" The kid's brows

pinched severely.

"Now we can't make it that easy for you." Mave opened the door as Logan began pushing Will in that direction, but the young guy braced his vivid pink shoes to counteract the progress.

"Dressed like this? I'll either get beat up or raped!"

"You're a fast runner, Bieb. All's good." Max couldn't resist getting in a snide remark about Will's tacky attire beings they dressed him something similar to that certain singer.

"Dad!" he whined, sounding like a frightened little boy trapped in a grown man's body.

Dillon started pulling on Will's arm as he said, "Welcome to the band, son."

"Seriously?" He tried wiggling his arm out of his dad's grasp, grunting as he fought against Logan's efforts.

"Pretty good initiation idea, Max," Dillon commented on a huff as he continued to wrestle with Will.

Will stopped fighting and threw his hands up in defeat, sweat trickling down his forehead as he cut a glare at his dad. "Fine! You know Momma is gonna lose it when she finds out about this." The others snickered and snorted at his futile attempt at sounding menacing, the faint tremble in his voice ruining it. He redirected his fury to the others. "Laugh it up, you punks. She ain't gonna let y'all get away with this either!"

That threat made them pause for a second before they all put effort into pushing him out of the SUV and onto his butt in the parking lot. As he stood up, they pulled the door shut and hit the locks. The guys cracked up as they sat there and watched him unsuccessfully try to cram the wallet into his too-tight back pocket.

"How in the heck did he get them suckers zipped?" Max asked.

All eyes were glued to the Will show. The frustrated guy waved the wallet in the air, gesturing wildly while his lips moved in a hasty tempo.

"Bet he's using lots of *nice* language," Blake said, releasing a deep belly laugh from the front passenger's seat.

"Alright, Sonny. Let's head out so he can get on with his little journey." Dillon's tone wasn't as laidback as before and he fidgeted a bit with discomfort.

"Our baby boy is gonna be just fine." Logan gave him a reassuring pat on the shoulder with Dillon relenting a hesitant nod in agreement.

As part of the plan, Blake reached over and cranked up the sound system to earsplitting. He then cracked the windows and opened the sunroof so Will could hear the selected song "On My Own" to inspire him.

Sonny put the SUV in drive. As he began to pull out of the lot, Will reared back and threw his wallet with all his might, hitting the darkly tinted window in an aggressive thud. The guys laughed all the way to the concert venue and continued reveling in the hilarity until they crossed paths with Jewels...

•♫•♫•♫•

Heavy bass thumped the arena as the opening act drove it home. The guys stood at the side of the stage watching the scholarship winners of their charity rock out. Gemma and the Gents was made up of college age guys with one lone girl, who was the lead vocalist. Gemma's voice was a powerful soprano that could rival in range with Adele. The day the Bleu guys listened to her for the first time, they were already blown away before she made it to the chorus of her audition piece. The raven beauty's talent would shoot her to the top and they were just happy to give Gemma and her band the sturdy foundation to take off from. The west coast tour was their introduction to the world, and from the sounds of the arena, the world was quite welcoming. The young band did remixes of Bleu Streak hits as the opener for the tour that night and the crowd seemed to love it.

"If he's not here in ten minutes, every one of you jerks will be finding a new home tonight!"

The guys reluctantly turned away from the show and regarded the petite blonde, her wavy long locks quivered with her wrath. Arms crossed, green eyes piercing each bandmate, there was no doubting she would follow through with the threat of kicking them out. She had already handed out a butt-chewing and a forceful punch to each one of their arms earlier.

Dillon tried to place his hand on his wife's shoulder, but she yanked away. "Will is fine—"

"How could you just abandon our child in the middle of nowhere?" Her wrath was steady building with each tick of the clock that showed up without any sign of her boy.

"He's a grown man, Pretty Girl."

"Don't you dare *Pretty Girl* me!"

Tate came closer while studying his phone. "He's only about five minutes out." He turned the phone so Jewels and Dillon could see the little red dot blinking as it moved closer to the arena.

"You're tracking him?"

"Yes, and Joe is following closely behind him." Dillon bent his knees to get closer to eye level with his wife, who was over a foot shorter than him. "Baby, he's going to be away at college in only a few short months. He's gotta get used to finding his own way around this life." He motioned around him as though the backstage held their entire world, but from the tears welling in her eyes, Jewels got it. He pulled her in for a hug, allowing his wife the moment she needed.

It was short-lived.

Busting through the side entrance sans purple tank top, Will sauntered over like nothing was amiss. "Yo, we ready to do this?" His cocky façade back into place.

Dillon looked up and grinned while Jewels pushed out of his arms. Her tears immediately ceased. "Dillon Dawson Bleu! His hair! And what on earth is our son wearing?"

"He had on a shirt when we left him." Dillon eyed his son. "Where's the tank top?"

"Some chicks said they'd give me a ride if they could have it with my autograph. Seemed a reasonable sacrifice." His lips tipped up.

Jewels moved closer to him to inspect the mohawk that was still holding its sharp form from the high-tech product the stylist used earlier. Will kept her to his left and when she leaned around the other side, he took to rubbing behind his ear and looking away.

"What's up behind that right ear, kid?" Dillon smirked when his words made Will squirm.

"Just a little itchy." He widened his blue eyes, relaying a silent message for mercy from his dad.

Dillon in reply narrowed his identical eyes with the message being clear he'd have to pay up later.

"Do you need some ointment? Let me see—" Jewels reached to remove his hand, but Will scooted away.

"Mom! It's fine. We gotta get on stage soon!"

Just then, the crowd erupted in applauses as the opening act waved and exited the stage, which effectively distracted the Bleu group. They offered the newbies fist bumps and words of encouragement as they passed.

"Will, you need to go change," Jewel instructed once they were alone again.

"He's already dressed." Mave grinned, but wiped it away when Jewels set a scowl in his direction.

She pointed without looking at Will's beyond-tight pants that showed not only the outline of his boxers but easily the black color of them. "Those are inappropriate on so many levels. I can't believe y'all dressed my son in such mess and let him parade around alone!" She turned to Tate. "Get him in something else or this show will have to happen with a one-armed drummer."

Izzy latched onto Will's arm, cheeks pink as she kept her gaze anywhere but on his pants and bare chest. "I'll help him find something." She passed Mave a stick of gum even though he wasn't set to perform but one song with Will as she hurried off with the oversized teen in tow.

"You guys owe me some Eddie Vedder tonight!" Jewels pointed at each member of the band. Bleu Streak would always come in second to Pearl Jam, and the guys had no other choice but to live with that.

They grumbled, knowing there would be no getting out of doing a cover song for her with what they pulled on her baby boy that afternoon.

"The show is going to start late and now you want to change the lineup?" Ben shook his head while running his hands through his salt-and-pepper hair. He and Tate ran a tight ship even though the Bleu guys never made managing them a cakewalk. At least they kept life interesting.

"What Pretty Girl wants, Pretty Girl gets," Dillon said before stealing a kiss from his reluctant wife. She continued to hold on to her frustration stubbornly. "I'll close it out with some Eddie. Promise."

"Two minutes to show-time," Blake said, glancing at his watch. He tapped a button on his headset before speaking into the small attached mic. "Stand by. May need a few more minutes."

"Just like you punks to hold up a show over silly shenanigans." Ben shook his head and began to pace.

Just as the two minutes were up, the sounds of a drum set coming to life drew the group closer to the edge of the stage. The spotlight flashed on to illuminate Will behind the set, going to town with his opener.

"He's wearing my change of clothes!"

Dillon growled out, shaking his head. Will was sporting his dad's blue T-shirt and dark jeans, but the gaudy pink sneakers were still on his feet. One worked the bass drum pedal as he jammed out, going through a medley of Bleu songs, weaving them in and out of one another.

"It was either that or he was stuck in those pants for the show. And those suckers had to be cut off." Izzy said, appearing out of nowhere. When the crowd glanced over their shoulders, her face warmed. She threw her hands up with her brown eyes flaring. "Tate cut him out. Not me!"

As Will concluded his solo opener, the crowd erupted, chanting his name. He stood in true rock-star fashion and flung his sticks into the audience before pumping his fists in the air.

"Come on before his head swells too much," Max said as he pushed past everyone and meandered onto the stage. As soon as the spotlight captured him, the crowd's ruckus rose another notch. He fist-bumped with Will and then backtracked to his spot.

The rest of the guys emerged in the same fashion, welcoming Will and then taking up their spots. When Dillon strolled out last, blue

Gibson strapped to his broad back, the cheers hit a crescendo. He waved at them as he strutted over to Will and commenced to picking the kid up like he weighed twenty pounds instead of two hundred. Still holding his son in a bear-hug hold, he walked to the front of the stage before releasing him.

"Nice kicks, kid," Dillon said, being sure to speak into the mic before him as he looked down at the outrageously bright shoes. The crowd roared and whistled while Will shrugged with indifference.

"They're doing their job." Will raised a leg and wiggled his foot around. "Like my threads, too, old man?" He smirked as he did a circle around with his arms spread out to the side to show off. Red-faced girls in the audience sounded close to losing their voices already with the screams pealing out over the banter between the two guys. Will was a natural in the spotlight, carrying an ease about him just like Dillon always possessed.

Dillon let his son's taunt go and directed his focus back to their fans. "So we decided it was time to make this kid an official member. Whataya think?" The arena erupted again, something Dillon Bleu was famous for instigating. He was enigmatic when on stage, and the fans thrived off his energy and he generously divvied it out.

"Sounds like a done deal. How 'bout we do some singing now!" Will shouted as a stagehand offered him his acoustic guitar. He quickly strapped it on and stood proudly by his dad.

The father/son duo began strumming the upbeat chords to Matthew West's "Day One" as the other band members clapped to encourage the fans to join in. Dillon noodled his chords over Will's lead, both heads bobbing in rhythm as they brought the praise song to vibrant life. The upbeat melody had the crowd dancing instantly. The two Bleu men crooned lyrics, declaring it was time to move forward and wanted to march to the beat of their own drum with the future finally beginning. Such an appropriate opening song to show the band's excitement for the launch of a new legacy—Will entering adulthood and taking a permanent spot in the band his dad formed in a shed back in a Georgia trailer park with secondhand instruments and a determined prayer.

The night rocked on with Will and Mave playing one of their epic drum highlights. This time Mave played the left-handed beats and

Will hit the right-handed ones as they shared the drums—the two guys syncing so seamlessly that it sounded as if only one drummer was owning the drums.

The energy was so vivacious, Bleu Streak allowed the chanting fans to talk them into two encores. When they erupted in demands for a third as the band departed to the back, Dillon pulled Jewels onto the stage with him.

After he placed her on one of the two stools he requested, Dillon addressed the audience. "I got some making up to do with my Pretty Girl. Y'all don't mind do ya?" This was another tradition the tattooed rock legend started way back when, and the fans always loved when they got to witness him serenade his wife.

Whistles and shouts rang out as he strummed his long fingers over the strings of his electric-blue Gibson, giving them time to settle back down.

"You see… Me and the guys pulled a few initiation pranks on Will today, and Jewels wasn't fly with it, so I've promised her a song from her favorite singer." He paused to wink at her. "Can y'all believe it ain't me?" Dillon shook his head in disbelief as he pushed his damp locks off of his forehead. He settled onto the stool and angled toward his wife as he strummed the strings of the guitar resting in his lap.

"You mess with *my* kid like that again and you'll not be my favorite anything," Jewels sassed, eliciting a round of laughter from the audience and causing Dillon to stop playing.

"Yes ma'am." Dillon grinned as he picked up her hand and touched her index finger to one of the strings. "Hold your pretty finger there for me."

Jewels nodded without question, knowing he wanted to her to participate in the song. As Dillon leaned closer to make his wife his only focus, his nimble fingers began to form the achingly sweet melody to "Just Breathe" by Pearl Jam, pressing her finger down on the string at the designated time.

The deep rasp of his voice captured the profound beauty of the lyrics as he gave them over to his best friend as a gift. Simple words that wisely held the understanding of how life is but a breath and one needed to realize the gift of people loving them. To just breathe it all in and not take it for granted.

"*Always stay with me. You're all I can ever see,*" Dillon crooned, changing the lyrics as he felt lead. He held his gaze tenderly to her eyes with reverent possession. She was all he could see, no doubt about it. There may have been thousands witnessing this song, but it was clearly meant for none of them.

"I promise to hold you until the day I die. And I promise I will on the other side…" He eased the song to a close before lightly placing his lips to Jewels—soft, slow, and beyond sweet.

As the audience came back to life in whistles and applause, the bubble Dillon formed around him and his wife evaporated.

"We only get one shot at this life. Make the most of it. Love with all of your heart. Chase your dreams with all of your might. And most importantly, honor God in *all* of it. Good night." He stood, entwined his hand with wife's hand and led her off the stage.

Late into that night, the keyed-up group rehashed the entire concert and jammed out with a few more songs on the first floor of the beach house. The guys wrestled around and cracked jokes past three in the morning, enjoying the wave of adrenaline coursing through their veins.

Max watched on from a corner of the long sectional coach with a content smile carefully held in place, hoping to hide the conflict twisting inside him.

"Dude, we killed it." Will was still bouncing off the walls. He tugged the edge of the beanie further down and caused it to sit cockeyed on his head, not wanting to expose the tatt to his mom just yet.

"You sure are cute, Beib," Mave teased while eyeing the odd getup Will had changed into after his shower. Teal plaid pajamas bottoms and those neon shoes rounded out his attire.

"Shut it," Will sassed back.

"You and Mave are like drum trapeze artists, ya know." Trace tried demonstrating by twirling a set of drumsticks in the air, but fumbled in catching them. Of course, one happened to track Mave down and smack him in the back of the head.

"Dude!" Mave rubbed the offending spot as he shot Trace a sharp look. "I think you meant jugglers, Space Cadet."

Trace continued on, looking mesmerized, "Y'all are more epic than mere jugglers. It blew my mind tonight how you never missed a beat and didn't drop a stick once."

"Our drum show was epic." Will offered Mave an exuberant slap on the back as he passed him to pick up one of Max's many guitars scattered around the room.

"Nah. You gotta hand it to your folks, man." Mave tilted his head toward the beach where Dillon and Jewels could be seen slow dancing under the dim moonlight. "Now those two are *epic* on a level unreachable. Dillon knows how to bring the house down."

"Truth," Logan said slowly, his head swaying to the quiet melody of the guitar.

Max's eyes wandered in the couple's direction along with the rest of the group. For the first time all night, the smile was genuine. No way could anyone not respect the epic love story out there on that beach. They loved each other wholeheartedly and didn't care who witnessed it. Dillon and Jewels made every minute count, knowing from a lesson learned the hard way to never take it for granted. The sudden stinging of his eyes caused Max to look away, knowing how badly he had failed. The smile slipped along with a rebellious tear as he snuck off to his room, hurrying away to hide his embarrassment over things he had no clue how to change.

THREE

"Steady As She Goes"
-The Raconteurs

The anticipated Music Festival Awards had everyone buzzing around in nervous energy. The women were fussing over what to wear and how to fix their hair. Of course, the guys were fussing over what the women chose for them to wear and how they wanted the guys' hair styled. All the while, the children ran around the house like it was one big jungle gym.

"Ludwig, take that out of your mouth," a sweet voice chimed over the ocean waves from the open windows.

Brooke and Logan had the harsh reality of not being able to have children confirmed the first year of their marriage, so they took to spoiling the ones around them. Brooke's mom Gayla had joined in and had designated herself as the band's nanny. She had become a Godsend when a pile of new babies showed up all at once. Grace grew quite attached to the spunky lady beings that she had no grandparents, so the preteen happily helped Nana Gayla with the little ones.

Even though Dillon's mom Cora was still living, she never tried mending a rip she inflicted in their relationship. After Dillon and Jewels tried and failed to make amends with her, they knew the only option was to knock the dust off their shoes and move on. God had richly blessed them with enough love and family to make up for it. In their world, there was no such thing as blood being thicker than water. The different ethnicities and backgrounds of the dynamic Bleu family was living proof of that.

Max sat on the back deck, avoiding the craziness inside the beach house as well as inside him. He strummed a tune on his vintage Martin acoustic to accompany the melody of the waves brushing against the shore. A few paparazzi cameras captured his quiet performance earlier, but had finally wandered away when he made no effort of doing anything in true Max fashion, like moon them or approach them and share a few stupid jokes. He kept his back toward them and offered no sign of acknowledging their presence.

"Alright, Molasses, you're about to get left." Mave strutted out, brown hair perfectly styled in disarray. He groaned in annoyance when he reached his twin who was dressed completely opposite of his sophisticated attire. "You ain't even dressed," he grouched out, motioning to Max's T-shirt and jeans.

"I'm a grown man. I can wear whatever I please." He lifted his shoulder slightly, a deflected habit that was starting to wear on his brother. "You can let the girls play dress-up with you all you want. I don't have to." He eyed the tailored button-down in a dark shade with the sleeves rolled up to show off the vivid canvas of ink displayed on Mave's arms. Brand new Vans peeped from under the hem of his perfectly pressed black slacks. The only rebellious touch was the studded belt with a chain dangling from it to the back pocket.

"Whatever. Let's hit it." Mave tilted his head toward the glass doors as he shoved his hands into his front pockets, drawing Max's attention.

"Where's your cast?" Max asked, already knowing the answer.

"It had to go. Couldn't let it cramp my style tonight." Mave pranced in a circle, hoping to get a smile to crack from his melancholy brother.

Max narrowed his eyes instead. "You've got another few weeks before that cast was supposed to come off."

"All's good. Are we picking up Mona?"

"I'm going to get her myself. We'll meet you there." He studied the strings underneath his fingertips before plucking a few chords from them, dismissing his brother.

"You sure?" Mave asked hesitantly.

"Yeah. Ben's lined it up."

"Okay… Meet you there, I guess." Concern whispered through his words, but Mave left it at that when Tate started hollering that it was time to go, followed by a horn honking from the front driveway. He glanced one last time over his shoulder as he reached the door. Max kept his face inclined to the guitar looking lost, and the guy didn't wear it well at all.

"I'll see ya there, dude," Max mumbled, apparently reading his twin's warring thoughts.

Mave cleared his throat and nodded before disappearing back inside.

After the house quietened, Max slowly gathered the guitar with enough courage to make it through the night and headed inside. Once he secured the old guitar into its original case—the second guitar he had ever owned—him and the guitar headed out to meet the waiting limo outside.

"Yo, Joe. What's up?" Max said as he slid onto the buttery soft leather seat, placing the guitar and a black fedora he had swiped on the way out of the door on the bench seat in front of him.

The driver glanced at him from the rearview mirror. "Hey, hey. Nothing's up except hauling your spoiled behind around tonight," he teased as he pulled the limo out of the gated drive.

"That's me, man. Totally spoiled. Thanks for putting up with me." Max managed a cocky smile as he pressed his damp palms into the cool leather seat. Unfortunately, it offered him no comfort.

"It's my pleasure, kid." Joe smiled as he focused on driving through the thick traffic. No matter how old Max and the others grew,

Joe seemed to still view them as the naïve punks that hired him after signing up for their first tour, still teenagers at the time.

Max knew Joe had to be getting close to wanting to retire and that only added to the pinch in his chest. He rubbed at it, begging for relief until they pulled up to the front entrance of the hotel. It was a posh establishment with lots of palm trees and thick foliage to shield it well from the outside world.

"Joe, you mind sitting tight a few." Max reached for the door handle. "I'm gonna—" Before he managed getting the door open or to finish his sentence, a stunning brunette angel began strolling toward the limo. The white goddess gown and gold stiletto sandals added to her ethereal appearance and completely stunned the guitarist.

"Stop drooling and go get your girl," Joe encouraged, chuckling at the awestruck man.

Max stumbled out and met Mona on the sidewalk. Her eyes clear and colorful as aqua sea glass met him openly, but Max noticed that the subtle lines around her large eyes were carefully holding an edge of pain. The delicate heels on her feet brought Mona to eyelevel with his six foot stature. Not able to stop himself, his nervous hand reached out to delicately brush the long silky curl off her bare shoulder. For the first time in months, he felt he could breathe, yet equally like he was drowning.

"I missed you," he whispered while taking more than he deserved, wrapping Mona in his arms. Inhaling the familiar coconut notes of her perfume, Max felt a protective surge to just grab her up and run away from life altogether. But when her hushed sniffle reminded him she deserved better, Max reluctantly let go and helped her inside the back of the limo. He climbed in the same side after she scooted over as far as the seat would allow.

"Good evening, Miss Mona," Joe said, giving her a big smile before putting the limo in drive.

She cleared her throat timidly. "Hi, Joe."

Her northern accent was so formal compared to the Bleu gang, but it had always been one of the unique parts of her Max found so appealing. He loved that he had rebelled against the group's preference to blonde southern belles with petite frames and had landed himself a Yankee brunette bombshell strong enough to kick his butt if need be.

Joe delivered Max a subtle nod of encouragement before he sent the privacy partition up between them, giving Max and Mona the moment they needed.

Mona nervously twirled the flashy diamond ring around her finger as she kept her eyes trained out the window and away from Max. He was relieved she was still wearing it. His body instinctively demanded he reach over and pull her close, but the stifling tension warned him to stay put on his side of the limo.

"You look beautiful," he murmured. The gauzy skirt of the dress touched the top of her tanned knees. She wrapped her hands there as though she could sense his gaze zoned in on that area. "Stunning," he reiterated, the rasp in his voice proving his sincerity.

Mona finally glanced over and studied him. His hand began easing over the long expanse of seat between them.

"And you look like you just rolled out of bed." Her words were delivered with no bite, just stating the obvious, but they successfully halted the progression of his hand.

Max moved back to his side, knowing it's what he deserved.

Scrubbing his hands over the stubble shadowing his jaw, he admitted, "I didn't feel like buttoning up in pretenses tonight."

"How ironic?" She huffed out a forced laugh.

"I know. Stupid choice of words." He grunted in discomfort. "I am who I am." He wasn't referring to his lackluster wardrobe for the evening. His composure began to slip and that starving kid screamed and begged for help. The haunted man knew if the layers of his defense were peeled back, it would reveal him bleeding profusely with regret so debilitating he felt his demise would surely follow.

"You are who you are," Mona echoed, eyes focused on her hands grasping a gold clutch in her lap as if it were a lifeline.

Max felt things slipping, so he demanded the shadows to retreat as he carefully resurrected his goofball façade, the lopsided grin guiding him into character. He knew he had no right to pull Mona down any farther than he already did.

"I'll have you know, sweetness, I did wash *and* put on deodorant." Max lifted his collar and sniffed dramatically. "And I'm pretty sure this is clean." The white V-neck tee was in stark contrast to his tanned arms and the black music notes of his only visible tattoo. The sheet music swirled up his right arm and disappeared underneath the short sleeve, but peeked slightly out at the base of his neck. He flexed his lean bicep when noticing Mona's focus was there. He ran his hand over his short hair, mussing it to stick every which-a-way. "Brushed my hair, too."

He received his desired effect, pulling a faint laugh from her coral glossed lips. Being able to offer her even the frivolous laugh empowered him to push a little more.

Leaning into her personal space, so close her stuttered breath touched his lips, Max whispered, "Glad I wore my boots, 'cause you looking so killer leaves no doubt I'm gonna have to kick the men away from you tonight." He licked his lips and winked. When her bronzed cheeks warmed with even more color, he couldn't help but reach over and brush his fingertips there to capture some of her warmth.

"Max…" Mona released his name on a lingering sigh.

The estranged couple overlooked the angst of their reality for a moment, both heartbeats fluttering under the other's touch and scrutiny. The tension pulled in another, more appealing, direction. Max cupped his hands gently under Mona's chin as his gaze drifted along her feminine features—high cheekbones, thick eyelashes, heart-shaped lips…

Something shifted between them, maybe a reality check out of the flirty delusional spell he tried weaving around them, as the lusty haze cleared from her eyes and left a watery sheen in its departure.

"Mona—"

"Please don't do this… I'm here because you asked. I've agreed to whatever you've asked… I just… I can't keep this up anymore. It's confusing… It hurts…" Her voice broke on a tremble, instantly cooling the heat between them.

The anger he had deliberately provoked in Mona months ago had evidently receded in his absence, leaving something in its wake that Max despised—pity. He saw it in her light-aqua eyes in that moment, knowing he deserved her wrath more so. She said it hurt, but the reflection only held pity…

He moved back over and said through gritted teeth, "I know. I'm a selfish bas—"

"Max!" Her eyes now held shock over his unusual outburst.

"I'm just stating the truth. A fatherless, self-centered punk is all I am. You deserve better." He kept his glare aimed at the guitar case across from him, knowing she wouldn't deny his claim of her deserving better. She did in the beginning, but he had told her enough that he thought she finally got it.

The limo pulled up to the black carpet that had silver music notes dancing along in a pattern all the way to the entrance of the substantial music hall. Max was livid with himself for casting such a dark mood on them only seconds before arriving. He grabbed the fedora and shoved it low on his head, wanting to hide from the undeserving sympathy she continued to offer him, even after what he had done.

Failure.

All I am is a failure…

The words had been on repeat in the back of his mind for the past year and revved back up as he trained his attention on the sea of people undulating with excitement.

"After tonight, baby, I promise you'll be free from all my madness." His words were muttered in defeat as Joe opened the door.

"Your guitar," Joe reminded as Max emerged from the backseat.

"Nah, man. It's all electric tonight. That's for later. Will ya keep an eye on it for me?"

"Sure," Joe responded, moving out of the way so Max could offer his hand to Mona as she stepped out of the back of the limo. "Always the gentleman your momma raised you to be." Joe smiled.

Max could barely muster a smile in response, knowing good and well his momma would knock him upside the head if she knew the mess he had made. Brushing the remorse off like a nagging fly that refused to completely go away, he eased a relaxed smirk on his face, knowing that's what the public expected from him. He lazily wrapped his arm around Mona's waist—a waist he just realized had withered to way too thin. The billowy layers of the dress had hid that tidbit well.

The onslaught of fans screaming out and the flashes of cameras engulfed them before they took a few steps. A few more steps and the barrage of questions began in a staccato chant to Max's ears.

"When's the wedding?"

A wry smile is all he offered in response as he ushered Mona forward. He paused to sign a few autographs for the fans enthusiastically reaching over the partition before moving on. The carpet felt miles long instead of yards.

"Are you taking home the Golden Guitar this year?"

"Straight up," he said over his shoulder to

the reporter, the shelf back in Georgia flinted through his head. It held five of the gaudy trophies already.

"Is it true that the two of you are already married?" another reported shouted out.

He gave the guy a shoulder shrug and smirk, knowing the media would draw their own conclusion on that one soon enough.

The questions continued, and Max continued to be blasé about it until one hit him like a hot skillet, searing every part of him.

"How do you feel about your estranged father checking back into rehab?"

Max froze for a split second, but felt Mona tighten her hold on his back, reminding him to keep moving. The lump lodged into the back of his throat, knowing he was freeing his anchor after tonight, and not knowing how he was going to survive without her. Thankful for just one more night, he brushed a kiss against her temple as they walked past the slanderous questions.

Ignore, ignore, ignore. He kept chanting this silently to himself until they finally reached the doors. Sweat trickled down his back, making him feel he had just crossed a firing line, barely dodging the bullets aimed right at his heart.

The cool, dark space of the building was

58

such a vast contrast to the tempest just outside. Max blinked several times, trying to adjust to it. He felt Mona move away from his grasp, but he instinctively clung tighter to her. Her stiff back relented, shoulders slumping just enough for only him to catch, as she allowed him to keep them tethered for a little longer.

An usher guided them past the marble lobby and on into the grand hall where everything was dripping in swankiness, from the crystal chandeliers to the fancy china dressing the tables. Max's stomach growled with remembering the main perk of the evening was they actually lavished decadent food on the guests instead of just the normal and disappointing alcohol. Drinking was something none of his crowd partook in.

They found the band gathered around a long velvet booth midway of the room. It was the VIP section and at a glance, Max noticed each of the long line of fancy booths held other performers for the evening's event. He nodded at few familiar faces, some already trash-talking about taking his title of guitar master this year. He donned the expected cocky grin and pretty much told the few rivals to "bring it on" as he swaggered on to his table.

Everyone stood, the women looking like

gorgeous blonde dolls and the guys looking like ultra-cool hipsters in their formal yet not quite attire. Each guy had the sleeves of their tailored button-downs rolled up, displaying colorful art on their forearms. Will was the only one with no ink, but Max had a feeling that was all in due time. The young member was proudly showing off the rebellious one behind his ear tonight with the mohawk spiked out of the way.

The girls attacked Mona first, wrapping the brunette in hugs, whining about missing her.

Jen perched her sassy hand on her sassy hip and glared at Max. "You need make more time for this chick. We miss her!"

Max ignored her and tried lightening things up. He pulled Mona out of Izzy's embrace and draped his arm over her shoulder before pointing at Dillon. "Dude has jeans on, too."

Mona easily played along with his light banter. "But there are no holes in his pair."

"Plus I'm wearing this hip vest with my dress shirt." Dillon smirked as he smoothed the front of the black suit vest that he had paired with a white button-down. The vest had a muted pattern on the upper right reminiscent of a tattoo design. Between that and his thick hair styled in a faux mohawk style, the rocker somehow pulled off an edgy formal appearance.

"But I'm sporting this swanky hat with my holey jeans." Max winked one of his dark-brown eyes at Mona.

The guys taunted one another for a little while longer as the hall seemed to reach full capacity. All the while, Max kept a firm grasp on Mona, needing his anchor. Everyone in their group had their acts together, but he still found himself flailing around in uncertainty. As he watched them chat and mingle so free-spirited, bafflement clamped his jaw firmly.

What is wrong with me? The words whispered through him.

Eventually, an announcer encouraged guests to find their seats and enjoy the meal before the festivities got underway.

Max helped Mona scoot in before taking a seat beside her, his hand not leaving her shoulder. He looked up and caught Dillon staring at him.

"What's up?" Dillon said, voice impassive yet all-telling.

Max played dumb and grumbled, "Food, I need food. Like yesterday." He needed to put something in his gut besides the aching dose of guilt and regret, so that he could to get through the next several hours.

Dillon kept his eyes trained on Max as he casually lifted a hand. The small gesture made a waiter appear instantly.

"Hey, my man," Dillon greeted. "We need some food."

"Lots of food," Max and Mave added simultaneously, pulling a needed chuckle from the group. It was obvious they had picked up on the tension Max and Mona brought along with them.

The night progressed on in a sluggish pace with eating lavish food, receiving a few coveted awards, watching performances, and then finally the anticipated guitar showdown. An attendant guided Max backstage where a bevy of people rushed around. Someone handed him his custom electric guitar he had specially made for this performance—the body glowed in gold metallic with a vivid blue outlining the curves of it. It made a statement and that statement pulled a wry grin to his face when he caught a few of his competitors eyeing the impressive instrument.

The announcer's voice bellowed from the speakers out front. "All right, ladies and dudes, who's ready to see if anyone can steal Maxim King's longstanding reign of Guitar King tonight?" His voice picked up volume at the end as the roar of the crowd got fired up.

"You punks know there's only one King here," Max declared with cocky attitude.

"We'll see about that," Ace, a lead guitarist from one of Max's favorite bands taunted back.

The half-dozen men standing in the dimly lit space, caught up with one another until a stagehand motioned them forward. Each took a designated spot on the stage, with instructions to move to the center when their time of five minutes in the spotlight came up. Max was in the middle of the lineup this year and he was relieved to not have to open nor close.

The energy vibrated on the darkened stage even before the first high-pitched sound was beckoned from the performers. Max adjusted the strap along his shoulder and pulled the brim of the fedora even lower just before the stage lights flooded him and the others in an array of techno color. And then the dam of talent burst forth as the first performer lit up his guitar with bright riffs. The guests erupted close to the stage, hands in the air, bodies thrashing in accord to the guitar shredding.

Max looked toward the middle of the vast room where he knew the judges, blindfolded and turned to face away from them, could feel the energy brushing against their backs from it being so tangible.

The next guy stepped forward, pierced and heavily tatted with his long hair completely shrouding his face. The intense sound reached up several biting levels as he amped it up, fingers working in rapid-fire along the fretboard.

With his head bobbing and eyes closed, Max let the aggressive sound take him away. The adrenaline began to course through his body well before his turn, sweat trickling down his taut back and a delicious hum building in his chest. Performer after performer showed their instruments who was boss, making the sounds submit at their fingertips.

By the time it was his go, music begged to be released from his soul. Without giving the audience any regard, Max began a hostile riff of his own, freeing it in almost an earsplitting scream from the instrument. He manipulated rage and passion from the strings, the two emotions tangling in a complicated force. As he moved to add a hot lick, the tempo changed without his permission. Gone were the violent chords, replaced by a bluesy melody so complex it confused even him. The guitar still wailed loudly, but the anger transformed to melancholy.

The crowd stilled instantly, spellbound in the emotions he elicited from the riffs. Despair, longing, bitterness, and perplexity merged in and out of the dramatic performance. Tears mingled with sweat as Max expressed just how he felt, knowing he could never put it into words. Music allowed a freedom of expression he had never found with anything else.

Max dug his fingers into the strings as forcefully as he could, yearning for the bite against his skin. He continued to play as he eased out of the spotlight to allow the next guitarist his time to shine. Even after the last note finished out, his fingers continued to grip the instrument to stave off a panicked tremor ricocheting inside him.

Without looking up to confirm, he felt eyes trained on him, even though his body was back in the shadows of the show. As the last musician concluded, the stage lit completely to cue the guitarists to finish out in a rehearsed performance, bringing the house down.

The judging was concurred before the

guitars hushed. The MC moved to the stage, carrying the coveted gold guitar trophy and a mic. He made eye contact with Max as he passed by. It was a look of wonder and respect. He spoke to the guests about it being the best guitar shred in history, and they all cheered their agreement. Max tuned it all out, still bewildered by his own performance that ended up being on the fly instead of the one he'd prepared.

The building erupted to a deafening leveling, pulling him out of his head. Looking around, all eyes were on him again.

"Do you want this or not?" the MC held up the trophy as he addressed Max.

Snapping to attention, he offered his lazy shoulder shrug and strutted to center stage. As he accepted the trophy, Max noticed Logan and Dillon lifting Mona to the stage. His heart sank seeing her hesitantly walk over to him, knowing she was doing all of this for him tonight.

Selfish…

So selfish…

Not allowing his spot-on thoughts to rob him of the moment, Max tossed the trophy toward Dillon with the giant of a man easily snagging it.

With both arms free, Max pulled Mona to him and whispered into her ear, "I'm so sorry," before dipping her and laying claim to her lips. Her posture remained stiff, but her hands laced around his neck anyway to allow him even more than he deserved.

The crowd erupted in catcalls and whistles, totally oblivious to the truth hiding behind the charismatic rocker's charade.

•♫•♫•♫•

Silence encapsulated the back of the limo with only the faint echo of passing traffic breaking through every so often. The ringing continued a languid vibration in his ears from the performance as Max reached for Mona's hand with her allowing it. He knew it was only going to make the sharp sting of him severing their ties that much harder. Mona knew, too, which made them both a masochist.

The imminent finality of their situation seemed to cause Mona to tighten her grip on his hand as she spoke, "Joe, do you mind dropping Max off first?"

Joe's eyes searched for Max in the rearview mirror. Max nodded his head, knowing they needed the privacy the beach house's gated drive would allow.

"Sure thing, sweetheart." Joe navigated to the right lane to begin the new trek.

They remained quiet until the limo was parked in the dark driveway.

"Give us a sec, Joe," Max muttered as he pulled Mona out with him. After closing the door, he pinned her to it and greedily inhaled her subtle scent, memorizing it.

"Max…"

He shook his head, keeping it burrowed to her neck. "This is too hard."

"But it's what you wanted."

He felt the tremble of her thin frame. His throat constricted painfully with knowing how much he truly loved her, but that just wasn't enough to push past the barrier he had constructed around his heart. No matter how much force Max inflicted through prayer and advice from his band family, the self-doubt and debilitating fear of abandonment refused to budge.

"I know… You deserve better," he repeated, holding her closer.

After he witnessed Mave get his act together and create a righteous life for his wife and kids, Max naively thought he could do the same with just as much ease as his brother. Without thought, he proposed to Mona and she agreed with no hesitation. All seemed to be on track until last summer when every cruel scar inflicted from his childhood made headlines.

"We can't keep doing this," Mona whispered, bringing his focus back to the night.

Blinking, he raised his head and met her watery gaze. "I know. Baby, I love you... I want you to have the world filled with sunshine... Never dark skies... I promise I'm done hurting you after tonight." He brushed his fingers over her delicate jawline. "I'm letting you go."

Her features plummeted even further, making him realize she was still holding on to some flimsy thread of hope. Mona took the diamond off and tried handing it over, but Max refused it.

"No. Please keep it."

"But it's gotten too big."

"What?"

Mona slid it back onto her finger to show how it dangled dangerously. "I've lost my appetite with everything going on..."

Max knew it was him who was the cause of the stress, reiterating the need to let her move on. It wasn't healthy to be with him. He slid the ring off and moved it to her index finger.

"There. It can be a statement ring." He inwardly flinched at his choice of words, knowing the only statement it conveyed was a broken engagement. Luckily, Mona pretended to overlook it.

She toyed with the silver guitar pick hanging on the long silver chain around his neck. It was one of the many gifts she had given him over the years. "Tell me..." She took a stuttered breath. "Tell me about your latest mischief."

Max knew she changed whatever it was she wanted to say, but he pretended to not notice. They had both become pretty good at playing along with the charade of their relationship. He gave in to temptation some more, allowing his hands free reign to play in her silky locks.

Pulling on a mischievous grin, he spoke, "Well, ole Dimples been going through some old-man faze of wanting to only wear white shirts." He wrinkled his nose in a silly fashion. "Weird, right?"

A weak smile pulled at Mona's lips as she nodded in agreement while eyeing the white shirt he himself was wearing that was still slightly damp from rocking out earlier. It was a bit loose around his abdomen but fit surprisingly well through the shoulders.

Max glanced down at the shirt. "This is actually his one and only white shirt as of today, but dude don't know it yet. Well, unless he wants to wear that fancy one he was sporting tonight."

"How's that?" Her smile warmed, hooking her fingers through his belt loops as his hands continued to work through her hair. The entire moment felt too familiar and too right with them easily falling back into couple-mode.

He released one hand and hiked up the left leg of his jeans to reveal splashes of pink along his shin. "I spent the morning adding some color back into his life."

She giggled, which successfully added some sparkle back to her sad eyes. "Seems you colored yourself."

Max dropped the leg of his pants. "Yeah. The bucket turned over on me. Jewels don't know it yet, but the lower deck has a pink section now. Maybe Leona can work that into her redesign." He grinned down at her. "Can't wait to see the dude's face."

At that, Mona's face fell, moving them back to the seriousness of their conversation.

"Max, you need to leave your childhood behind." Before he could retort, she plowed on. "I'm not talking about the goofing off or the pranks. Never lose your sense humor and mischief. Just please figure out how to stop using it as a shield."

Max cleared his throat, trying to push it all back down, but her words had wiggled the wayward hurt loose and it threatened to overtake him. He was about to let her go, but her hand moved to rest over his pounding heart.

"Whatever broke your heart back then needs to be fixed, or you'll never be able to get over it properly." Her fingers tapped against his chest. "I've gotten a glimpse of that love when you let things go. And I know if you ever heal, that love is going to be one spectacular prize for some lucky girl."

He had no words for that, so his head nodded in acknowledgement but not agreement. The broken guitarist just didn't know if he was capable of offering anyone anything spectacular. But that was always Mona. She always saw the best in people, and that's why she made one outstanding publicist.

Mona placed a kiss on his cheek. "You need to grab your guitar."

"No. That's for you."

Her eyes snapped up to his. "But that's your first acoustic. I can't… That's too…"

"That's why I want you to have it. Baby, I promise…" He sniffed his traitorous tears back, his brown eyes burning. "I need you to understand… It's the only way I can figure out how to show you how much it's killing me to part with something so precious to me."

"Then I'd rather you keep it." Her own tears brimmed until finally spilling.

Max pulled her closer. "I'm talking about you, not the guitar."

A sob pulled from her, weak and tortured. Max leaned down and allowed his tears to mingle with hers as he gently laid his lips to hers. Poignant and heart wrenching was how the caress began, but it moved aggressively on to need and longing. By the time they parted, both were panting.

"If chemistry were enough to fix my stupidity… 'Cause, baby, we've got that in spades."

Mona freed a slight laugh. "Sounds like song lyrics to me." She leaned up and pressed one final kiss to his lips before climbing into the limo. "Let me know when you're ready to release a statement."

"Only thing I'm releasing is you for your own good," he muttered, knowing she couldn't hear him with her head turned away. Max leaned down and summoned her to look at him, stealing one last inhale of her sweet scent. "I love you, you know that, right?" He gathered the new tear his words beckoned with his thumb before it slid down her damp cheek.

"I think I do." She didn't offer him the same declaration. Mona had always been firm on showing someone how she felt instead of saying them. She proved her love by showing up tonight to make a public appearance easier on him. And she also showed it by putting up with him for over six months after he called off the engagement.

Max quietly shut the door and watched the limo disappear into the summer night. A long time passed with him standing in the dark driveway, coming to terms with just how messed up he truly was at that point in his life. He wished he could fix the effect his past had on him. His dad walking away from them, not caring how they survived, had really screwed up his thinking on commitments and had rooted a deep abandonment phobia.

"Yeah. Not happening," he muttered to the

night sky, not knowing how to fix any of it. He turned his back to the sky after it offered no resolution.

FOUR

"Tiptoe"
-Imagine Dragons

The perpetual chatter and commotion bounced around the rambunctious beach house. The sounds were ever-present and could almost soothe anything ailing you, but the profound hole in Max's stomach throbbed with needing to be filled with more. A few days had dragged by with him hiding out, but he reemerged back into the chaos of his family. A concert was scheduled for that night, plus Kyle and Leona's crowd were expected to arrive, so he knew it was time to push down his wallowing over screwing everything up with Mona.

Scratching at the thick scruff on his cheek while perched on a stool at the kitchen island, Max knew exactly what he needed for a brief cure of what was ailing him. The antidote taunted him from the warm glow of the oven.

Jewels rushed by, arms filled with freshly laundered linen. "Izzy, I'll take care of the beds."

"Okay. I'm almost finished baking," Izzy called out from the sink, but Jewels had already disappeared up the backstairs.

Max remained zoned in on the heavenly treats perfuming the air—peaches shipped all the way from Bleu Orchard, sugar, a hint of spice, and buttery crust. If he focused there, the leering thoughts of missing Mona would take a rest. Will's large form came barreling through, holding a cellphone over his head with Grace hot on his heels, jolting Max out of his pie lust.

"Give it back!" the raven beauty screamed before they disappeared into the living room.

"This sure ain't a vacation. Every five seconds someone's dancing around in a tizzy." Max frowned deeply, moving his hands to rub through his messy hair. It was starting to get some length back to it.

Izzy turned and studied the brooding guitarist. The two of them had a love/hate relationship, but the hate thing was all for show. He knew she was watching him, but Max had no desire to look anywhere but toward the enormous oven holding lots of pies. He licked his lips and swallowed. *She won't miss one pie…*

"Don't even think about it, Pepper Man," she warned, narrowing her brown eyes.

Oh, he was thinking about it, all right, and had a plan in place to snatch a pie as soon as she gave him an opening. He'd pay whatever consequences, because one of those pies was his whether Izzy was ready to admit it or not. His sister-in-law had sufficiently shed her shyness over the years, discovering a confident woman underneath. Max thought she wore that look brilliantly. It definitely kept him on his toes. Snatching the pie wouldn't be an easy feat, that's for sure.

Max swallowed forcefully again, stomach growling its irritation for having to be patient. "When did you say the crowd was arriving?"

"I think they are actually flying out together." She glanced at the wall clock. "In about an hour."

"Sounds good." An hour to enjoy his pie sounded *really* good. "I'm glad Kyle was transferred to New York right after Grant's death. I didn't like the idea of Leona and Phoebe out there alone."

"Me too." Izzy nodded her head somberly with wisps of almost-white-blonde hair escaping her topknot. She worked on washing several heads of romaine lettuce, blowing the wayward locks out of her eyes every so often. "I wonder what she has in mind for the remodel."

They both glanced around the room that held a beach décor scheme, but nothing garish. It was a classic beach style bathed in creams and beiges with accents of blue, but the dynamic view of the Pacific Ocean showcased by the floor to ceiling windows was most definitely the highlight.

Max shrugged. "I don't see anything wrong with the way it is now. I think Jewels used that as an excuse to get Leona for the summer. Those two were inseparable back in the day."

"Will Mona be coming by before the concert?" Izzy asked hesitantly.

"She's already back on the East Coast." His eyes suddenly stung, wishing he could confess what he had done to someone.

"That's one busy lady." The petite woman glanced over her shoulder.

Clearing his throat, Max muttered, "Yep," deciding he wasn't up for a confession.

Squeals pealed out as Trace's two boys ran through the kitchen in swim trunks with floaties strapped around their upper arms, followed by their dad. They waved new pool noodles in the air like swords, knocking into Max's back as they passed. Roland wasn't paying attention and ran smackdab into the glass door. He ricocheted off, but didn't let it deter him from his quest of getting to the pool. He shot through the door as soon as Trace hurried over and opened it.

"We need to call him Space Cadet Junior," Max mumbled. Trace cut him a look before following behind his boys.

"Why don't you go join them?" Izzy insisted.

"Nah. I'm good right here." No way was Izzy going to distract him from his pie mission.

Max glanced outside to where most of the crowd was already frolicking in the pool. His stomach tightened as he watched Mave pick Ludwig up and toss him to the other end of the pool, causing a big splash. Max almost got off the stool, but saw Dillon was right there to catch the little tyke.

Izzy said something he didn't catch before

she started rummaging around in the industrial-sized fridge. It was new as well as the rest of the appliances—stainless steel and smudge proof—and she seemed to make it her mission to break them in during their summer stay. The crowd had no problem with that. Max made quick note on the location of the new jug of milk—top shelf on the left—before she shut the door and made her way back to the island with several cucumbers in her arms. A spoon was already hidden in the back pocket of his baggy cargo shorts.

"You know your idiot husband is supposed to be taking care of that arm. Slinging toddlers in the pool ain't doing it."

"Go out there and get ahold of him."

Before Max could decline, a beautiful sound tickled his ears.

Finally! Finally, the timer went off on the oven.

Max reined in his exhilaration over the beeping that exclaimed in a high-pitched inflection that he was finally about to have his pie and eat it too. As Izzy began pulling the pies out of the oven and lining them neatly on the cooling racks sitting on the island, Max casually strolled over to the glass doors to prepare for his plan of action. He feigned interest in the craziness happening in the pool, but his entire being was zoned in on the potent perfume of the peach pies that became almost overbearing now that they were free from the confines of the oven.

"What kind of salad are you making for lunch?" he asked nonchalantly.

"Chicken curry."

"Hmm… That sounds good. Do you mind chopping up some pickles like I like them to go with it?"

"Sure."

Max waited to hear the door to the fridge open before yanking the glass door open in sudden panic. "Mave! Pearl can't swim! Get her!" His voice rang out in hysterics, reaching pretty high for a baritone.

Mave looked up in confusion at his brother like Max had grown another head. Pearl was latched onto his back as he walked around the shallow end of the pool while pulling Ludwig on a float. Only seconds ticked by before Izzy dashed out the door, almost knocking Max down. With her nicely distracted and outside, Max quickly slid a steaming pie off the rack with a pot holder. Set on his path of escape, he swiped the milk from the fridge and hauled tail to his room.

Feeling as though he just pulled off some high-stake crime, heart thumping rapidly in his chest and sweat dampening his forehead, Max locked himself in and settled on the floor beside the unmade bed after kicking a few articles of clothing out of the way. Taking a few calming breaths, he began working the spoon into the top crust that was browned to golden perfection. Before he could deliver the bite to his salivating mouth, a harsh beating attacked his door.

"Maxim King! So not cool!" Bang, bang, bang. "Stealing a pie by making me panic over my child!" Bang, bang, bang. Each of her words was delivered along with a fist to the door.

He eyed the gooey fruit and crust on the spoon with wafts of steam rising. "It's good to keep you on your toes with the rugrats," he hollered back before taking the first bite, dropping his head back to rest on the bed and moaned. "Dang, this is good!" he garbled out.

"You forget too easy what happens when you mess with me, *Pepper* Man!" Izzy let the threat drip through the word pepper, sounding right menacing for such a tiny woman.

Her threat caused the spoon to waiver a split second at his lips. Shrugging, he took another bite and slowly chewed. "This pie will be worth the consequences!"

She kept up the attack on his door and the knob. "Max!"

"Go away!" he yelled back.

Izzy's tirade lasted until half the pie had vanished before finally giving up. With the peace and quiet settling around his dark room, Max tucked into finishing his pie mission. He cocooned in the shaded corner, lucky to have the first floor bedroom. The deep-blue walls helped to tone down the bright light flowing in from the large windows. Not once during daylight hours had he flipped on a light switch.

By the time the dish was empty and the jug of milk drained dry, Max declared the mission a success. With heavy eyes from the sugar high, he debated climbing back into bed. His hand was on the rumbled cover to push it out of the way when ruckus broke loose from above, signaling the arrival of his friends. Looking at the bed with longing one last time, Max unlocked his door and headed upstairs.

Keeping his eyes peeled for Izzy, Max stepped into the living room and stumbled upon an odd mix of shock and awkwardness. Everyone was perched on the cream-colored couches and chairs, staring in the same direction. Max angled his head and caught sight of Kyle. Features of the kid he had grown up with mingled with the mature version—the unruly dark-blond hair was now neatly trimmed with a few specks of grey and those light-green eyes were framed with a few fine lines.

"What's happening, man?" Max pulled his friend out of the chair and wrapped him in a bear hug, choosing to ignore whatever he had missed for the time being.

"I got married," Kyle blurted with genuine happiness.

Guess there's no ignoring it now, Max thought as he pulled back to eye Kyle.

"Woo... Wow. Well, congratulations. When do we get to meet the lucky girl?" Max glanced around the room and only saw one stranger's face, too young for his friend, so obviously she was Leona's assistant. His focus landed on Leona, pulling a wide grin to his face. "Hey, hot mama!" He forgot about Kyle's sudden nuptials and swooped his other friend up.

"Look at you," Leona said on a giggle. "You don't look wormy anymore."

"'Course not. I'm sexy now, ain't I?" He

grinned, brown eyes dancing in tease. "Ya looking good yourself." He took his time studying her, happy that time seem to be healing her. Gone were Leona's long dreadlocks, replaced by an asymmetrical bob with a rich brown hue near the roots and gradually lightening into a blonde at the tips. She was the group's designated hippie growing up, and from the flowy sundress and Birkenstocks, she still fit the bill.

"What's all this?" she questioned, rubbing her palms over his facial hair.

"Beards are in, didn't you know?" He winked, fully enjoying the light banter after dwelling in such darkness for the last several days. He leaned in, and whispered not quiet enough, "Please tell me Kyle didn't knock up your assistant and then marry her."

The room erupted into laughter, cutting some of the tension. Leona laughed along with them before reining it in so she could answer him. "No. He married me, but I'm not pregnant."

"Wha?" He looked at her dumbfounded for a few beats before glancing over at Kyle, who was grinning like a Cheshire cat.

Leona stepped back and wrapped her arm around her teenage daughter, a sad smile brushed along her lips as Kyle joined in wrapping his arm around Phoebe. "Kyle has really been there for us the last two years."

The room digressed back to that confused state he shuffled in on only minutes ago.

It looked like Kyle and Leona had some explaining to do.

• ♫ • ♫ • ♫ •

Jewels paced the master bedroom, the creamy whites and blues matched the rest of the beach house color pallet. She had decided it was time for a change last fall and it took until the spring to convince Leona to take the renovation on. The petite blonde shook her head, causing the long, wavy locks to tumble around her down-casted face.

Dillon stepped in front of her, halting the progression of her worrying steps, and brushed the hair away from her face. His large hands cupped her cheeks and tilted her head so that she had no choice but to allow him access to her green eyes.

"Talk to me, Pretty Girl." The deep rumble of his voice soothed her instantly.

"I'm just... I don't know how I feel about this."

"At least you didn't react how Kyle did when he first found out about us." One of his dark brows lifted, charming her right into a low chuckle.

Kyle had handled his shock by giving Dillon a bloody lip. That was a New Year's Eve to not be forgotten. They were only teenagers back then, but they were adults now and if Kyle and Leona were happy, then Jewels would get used to it.

"No, I'd never punch her. I just never would have guessed Kyle had been in love with her all these years."

Her younger brother admitted how he'd loved Leona his entire life to the entire group downstairs earlier, shocking them all again. Not even Leona had known his feelings until last year. Kyle put in the transfer so that he could be there for Leona and Phoebe after Grant's passing. He had no intentions of pursuing her romantically, just wanted to be there for her to lean on. But the more time they spent together, the more she began to reciprocate his feelings.

Dillon eased over to the foot of the California-king bed and pulled Jewels along with him until she was straddling his lap. "I think best friends make the best life partners."

His words were muffled as he coasted his lips along her neck.

"You do, do ya?" she teased while playing in his thick black hair.

The forceful Italian blood coursing through his veins seemed like a fountain of youth, no wrinkles and no greys dared mess with the enigmatic Dillon Bleu. He carried such a youthful soul, as well.

He growled slightly, pulling her snuggly against him. "Absolutely. Look how well we fit together."

The heat between them escalated as their lips crashed together, but before Dillon could deepen the kiss, the door flung open.

"Ah gross! Can't you two ever knock that stuff off?" Will's upper lip curled in revulsion.

"Perhaps you need to learn to knock first, kid." Dillon leveled his son with a warning look that clearly said to get lost, but Jewels was already climbing off his lap before he could stop her.

"What wrong?" she asked, settling beside her irritated husband on the bed.

Will scratched the back of his neck and focused on his more welcoming parent. He tried not to dwell on the fact that her hair was a hot mess. Shaking his head and clearing unwanted images away, he said, "Max is acting weird."

"What's new with that?" Dillon leaned his elbows on top of his knees and interlocked his fingers, his rigid demeanor was clearly not welcoming.

"More than normal. He's down in the basement, staring at his guitars like they might have some answer he's searching for." His brows furrowed together, clearly worried about his friend.

Dillon shrugged. "They just might. How about go down there and ask him to teach you a new riff or break or *something*."

Will eyed his dad knowingly. "You're just trying to get rid of me."

"Straight up," Dillon admitted with no hesitation. "I'll check on Max later. Now get out."

With a huff and a wagging finger toward his parents, Will said, "You two behave yourselves." He slinked back out the door, closing it a little too sharply behind him.

Dillon hopped up and locked the door before pulling his shirt over his head and tossing it behind him. His hair perfectly mussed and a devilish smile showcased his dimples.

"What are you up to, Dimples?" Jewels giggled as she watched her handsome husband stalk in her direction, kicking off his shoes in the process.

Mischief twinkled in his nearly purple eyes as he worked his belt loose. "I don't feel like behaving."

"No?" Jewels asked, heat traveling up her neck as his strong hand landed there, feeling her pulse flutter.

"Not even a little," he said before reclaiming her lips.

• ♫ • ♫ • ♫ •

Will found Max in the same state he had left him, sitting on the couch staring at the guitars displayed before him.

"What's up, hotshot?" Will plopped down beside him and fixed his eyes on the red Gibson. It was a custom design that Max got to do a few years back. The same sheet music tattoo whirling up his arm also whirled up the white fretboard. "I'm taking that one." He nodded his head toward it.

That seemed to snap Max out of his trancelike state. He blinked before focusing on the Gibson in question. "The heck you are."

One sure thing about Maxim King was he was deftly possessive over his beloved guitars, never parting with them easily. At least twenty or so always traveled with him on tours.

Will stood and gathered two acoustics, leaving the red beauty on the stand, and handed Max one before settling back on the couch. He strummed a few chords. "Teach me something, ole wise one."

Max snorted. "So you can steal my place in the band?"

"You old geezers will have to retire one of these days. Might as well impart your mad skills on me before arthritis settles into your decrepit fingers."

"You got such an arrogant mouth on ya." Max narrowed his glare at Will and held it there while his fingers brought the strings to life in a rapid melody, making it impossible for Will to catch the order of the chords.

"Alright, wise guy. You made your point. Now teach me that."

The two sat on the couch for a long stretch with Max patiently showing Will the riffs. Oddly enough, the guitars seemed to bring him out of his funk.

"What's wrong, young whippersnapper?" Max mimicked an elderly voice while he watched Will flex his fingers, knowing he made another point that his fingers wouldn't be slowing down any time soon.

"Nothing," he muttered, dropping his hands in his lap.

Max rose, stretched his back, and moved to place the guitar back on its display. "I'm starving."

Will snorted. "Nothing new there." He put away his guitar as well, standing several inches taller than Max's six-foot stature. "Izzy has a salad made."

"It's wise for me not to be eating anything from Izzy for a while." He slid a pair of flip-flops onto his feet while shoving his wallet into the back pocket of his shorts.

"What did you do now?" Will watched him curiously.

That twitchy shoulder shot up in a shrug as he said, "I sorta gave her a scare with one of her kids so I could steal a pie. She wasn't cool with that."

"I bet not. Where are you heading?"

"I want a hot dog." Max shoved a set of keys in his pocket before pulling on a lightweight plaid shirt with a country western flair to it. He unrolled the sleeves and buttoned the pearl snaps at his wrists to conceal his tattoo.

"Pinks?" Will asked and Max nodded. "That's a bit of a haul from here. How are we getting there?"

"I've got a set of wheels, but who said you were invited?" He lifted a brow at the kid he'd witness grow before him over the years into the too-sure-of-himself man.

"Come on, man. Let me go with ya."

Max didn't know why Will was all of a sudden attaching himself to him like white on rice, but he had no real reason to refuse the kid a slamming hot dog. "Meet me in the garage. Hurry it up."

Those long legs had already disappeared upstairs before Max finished speaking. Will yelled from above, "Sweet. Let me grab my shoes."

A few minutes later, Will rushed in the garage nearly out of breath, but froze at the new addition to the auto collection. In the midst of three sleek SUV's, one top-of-the-line Jeep Wrangler, and a half dozen shiny Harleys sat an outcast.

"Dude, tell me you didn't buy this piece of crap." Will wrinkled his nose while eyeing the rusted late-model pickup truck. Hints of baby-blue peeked out in a few spots, letting it be known that at one point there had been actual paint on the beat-up body.

Max moved to the driver's door. *"Language,"* he mock-scolded, allowing plenty of sarcasm to coat the word. His eyes went wide with bogus outrage.

"Man, if that's the worst I ever say," Will retorted.

"Ya preaching to the choir on that one, kid." Max held his hands up lazily.

Will circled around the poor excuse for transportation. "Seriously, why this?"

Max pulled two worn cowboy hats out of the back. "What happens when we parade around in your pop's tricked-out Escalade?"

"Lots of attention."

"Yep. He's broadcasting. I ain't feelin' up to that today."

"I get it." Will nodded his head.

"Good. Then get in and let's go." He tossed one of the hats and Will caught it one-handed.

"What's with the hats?"

Max shoved the other straw hat on low and refrained from rolling his eyes at the kid's naivety. "To hide your purdy mug. Come on, man, wake up and stop with all the questions."

"Oh," Will drawled out as the lightbulb blinked on with understanding. Shoving the hat on low, Will plopped onto the vinyl seat and slammed the door, leaving a dusting of rust on the garage floor.

Max slid in and after trying to start the engine a few times, the truck coughed heavily to life. He worked on syncing his phone to the impressive sound system that was way out of place and clearly a new addition. A few moments later, heavy guitar riffs filled the cab of the truck, then the heavy bass kicked up to rattle the windows.

"'Santa Monica'? Really?"

"Straight up. Everclear should be on your playlist as a lyrical lesson." Max turned the volume up even louder as one of his all-time favorite bands crooned out in a harsh declaration of wanting to find themselves a new place and wanting to see some palm trees.

The ancient pickup truck puttered down the Santa Monica Boulevard, owning it. Both cowboy hats ticked to the thick beat Everclear delivered as the guys sang along to the top of their lungs, releasing pent-up frustrations in a creative way until they were close to becoming hoarse.

Halfway to the best hot dogs on the planet, both guys morphed back to just listeners. The more relaxed expression on Max's face from their earlier jam session began to harden again, lines forming along his brow with lips pressed firmly together. Now his eyes were trained on the palm-tree-lined boulevard as though it may have held the answer he needed.

Will kept stealing side glances, worrying the mood would carry to the stage that night. He wished Max would talk to him. Nervous to broach the subject, Will decided to try another approached as he leaned forward to turn the music way down.

"Stella is *hawt*! I ain't ever seen grey eyes like hers before."

"Who?" Max mumbled distractedly, not taking his attention off the road.

"Leona's assistant."

Max finally glanced over, but quickly went back to studying the highway. "Ain't she too old for ya?"

"Nah, man. She's only three years older.

"Like father, like son." Max snorted.

"Mona is older than you, too. Only by a few months, but still..." Will threw it out there, but wished he hadn't when Max's face crumbled. Clearly, the problematic nail had been hit on the head. "What's up with you?"

Max worried his thumbnail between his teeth, not wanting to answer, but the burden weighed too heavy. "We split." His voice barely had enough volume to confess the two words, but from Will's quick intake of breath, they were received.

"That sucks, man."

"No doubt."

"Wanna talk about it?"

Max left his nail alone and shook his head. "Nah. Right now I just want to eat a hot dog." He pulled into the busy little place, lucking up with actually finding a vacant parking space. Max left his funk in the cab of the truck, and sent out a challenge to Will as he slid on a pair of Logan's aviators wanting to blend in more. As they stood in line, Max nudged Will's arm with his.

"What?"

"Hot dog eating contest. Winner gets the Gibson."

Will was naïve enough to think he had a shot at the coveted guitar and shook Max's hand automatically. "You're on."

Max grinned knowingly as he ordered two dozen chili dogs and two large sodas. Maybe he could push down the hurt clawing at his gut with the food and a little friendly competition since the pie didn't cut it earlier.

The guys were actually able to go

unrecognized. The only odd looks they received were over the obscene amount of hot dogs they ordered and then commenced to devouring. In the charismatic world of Maxim King, he declared it a successfully normal afternoon…

Or it was until he had to park in the median on the boulevard so Will could puke underneath the sparse shade of a tall palm tree.

Leaning out the truck as he pushed down on the rusty horn, Max hollered, "Come on, lightweight! We gotta hit it!"

Will shuffled back to the truck and slowly slid back inside. The rest of the trip back to the beach house was filled with miserable moans and gagging.

Later on, Max strolled up the back deck of the beach house where everyone was gathered. They all seemed ready for the concert and were just catching up with Leona and Kyle. Seeing the newly married couple caused his heart to squeeze in pain, reminding Max of how he had squandered his chance.

"Hey, hey," Trace welcomed, drawing Max's unfocused attention.

"Yo," he muttered.

"Where have you been and where's Will?" Jewels demanded while braiding Grace's long black hair.

"We grabbed some hot dogs." As Max eased over to the deck table the sounds of violent retching came from the side of the house. "He's okay. Thought he could out-eat me. Guess that's a lesson learned."

Jewels was instantly up and out of her chair, but Will came around the corner looking pale before she got too far. "Will, you should have known better than to try out-eating Wormy."

"Hey!" Max spoke up, while gesturing to his not-wormy physique. Jewels glared at him, so he thought it best to let her slide.

Will moaned as he staggered into the house with Jewels following him. "Let's get you some antacids," she offered along with a pat on the back.

"Thanks for the invite," Mave snapped.

"Figured you were busy eating salad." Max gave Mave a wry smile, causing his brother to reciprocate it with a punch in the arm.

"Not cool," Mave muttered, heading inside as well.

"How many dogs did Will eat?" Dillon asked, his feet kicked up on the deck table with his hands laced behind his head. Always laidback.

"I think he managed about nine."

"And you?" Logan asked, mimicking Dillon's pose on the other side of the table. His aviators concealing the amusement twinkling in his golden eyes.

"Thirteen, but then I grabbed a few more for the drive home." Max shrugged before heading in to shower, leaving the guys chuckling.

FIVE

"Mess Around"
-Cage the Elephant

"What If I"
-Meghan Trainor

Tate pushed through the guarded door of the green room that was actually grey. He found the band hanging out as they always did before a concert. Three black leather couches and a few plush chairs were occupied by the guys as well as Blake and Ben. Both Mave and Will were using a set of barstools as makeshift drums while the others watched on. The family had already been escorted to the VIP section up front of the arena to catch the opening show, so now was the bands calm before the show.

Well, that was the plan...

"Interview time. Max, you may want to put a shirt on," Tate said, eyeing the half-dressed guitarist, also noticing no shoes were on his feet.

Max looked up from the guitar he was lazily strumming. "Why's that?"

"This is a live interview for *Entertainment Now*, and they want to feature you." Tate picked up the shirt resting on the arm of Max's chair and signaled for him to put it on.

"Why's that?" Max repeated, not making a move for the shirt.

"You just stole the show at the music festival with that mind-blowing performance. *Why* else?" Tate rolled his eyes, his annoyance prevalent with the wickedly talented guitarist still not comprehending it. The entire band, for that matter, didn't get the ramifications of their talent. Not even multi-platinum records, #1 hit songs, and a treasure trove of awards seemed to make it clear about the level of fame they had earned over the years.

"Get the shirt on," Ben spoke up as he tossed Max his abandoned pair of Converses.

"Yes, sir," Max mocked as he pulled on the black V-neck shirt and shoved his feet into the shoes. He reached behind him to retrieve the black fedora from the floor and shoved it low on his head using it as a shield for his eyes and the bad case of bedhead he was sporting. His palm tested the side of his jaw, thankful some scruff remained even though Jewels and Izzy held him down earlier so the stylist could give it a good trimming.

"The reporter has been warned not to go near personal," Tate said with a reassuring nod as he moved back to the door.

"Yeah, but since when do they ever listen," Max grumbled, slumping down even further, wishing the suede chair would swallow him on the spot.

"Who's the reporter?" Dillon asked, his brow pinched with concern.

"Vee Declan," Tate answered hesitantly.

Groans and grunts moved through the group.

"You guys don't have to stay," Ben spoke up while glancing over the schedule attached to his clipboard.

"Yes, we do," Dillon answered for them all. No one made a move to leave, all nodding their heads in agreement.

After Will recovered from the hot dog binge from earlier, he pulled the group downstairs where they had an impromptu meeting with Max. One thing the band had made clear from the get-go is that they couldn't keep secrets from one another. It was the only way to truly have their mate's back, so Max knew as soon as they crowded around him that Will spilled the beans on the break-up. He wasn't upset about it, because Will was only doing what was deeply ingrained in him to do. Max asked that they just let him be about it for the time being, and Dillon said he knew where they were when he needed them.

So they were right where he needed them when the audacious host pranced her unwelcomed self through the door. Red hair with signature hot-pink streaks and a skintight teal dress reminded Max of an anorexic clubbing Barbie. She set her overly done eyes straight on him and sashayed in his direction as the small camera crew began setting up in front of the chair that refused to swallow him.

"Just the man I need to see," Vee flirted, voice pitching a bit too high from her fake enthusiasm.

As she drew near, Max heard Mave humming the song, "Mess Around" by Cage the Elephant while tapping a drumstick against the armrest of his chair. The suitable lyrics began playing through his mind.

Oh no… She'll drive ya crazy… No, she don't mess around. She comin' for ya. Gonna break ya. Ah, oh no.

After shooting Mave a look that said, *you got that right*, he reluctantly stood and shrugged on his best Maxim King impersonation. "Hey, sweet thang."

The flirty host went in for a hug, but Max managed to dodge most of it with only a side-hug before launching himself back into his chair. He quickly pulled the guitar back on his lap as a buffer against any more of her unexpected advances.

"Vee, just want to remind you of what we've already discussed," Tate said firmly.

She turned and barely refrained a glare. "Of course, hon. Max knows I'm his good friend." She redirected her focus on the man in question and gave him an exaggerated wink.

"Good. Let's get going. The guys only have a few minutes to spare."

"Just waiting for the cue from my producer."

Vee made a speedy trip around the room to flirt with each band member and offer unreciprocated hugs. Once done with the greetings, she took the seat a crew member had set up in front of Max and began reapplying bright-pink gloss to her already lacquered lips.

Vee was one of those Hollywood vixens the guys had deemed full of venom and did their darnedest to steer clear of her malice line of vision. If Max were in a better place in his life, he had no doubts the guys would have bailed as soon as the trifling woman's name had been mentioned.

"Thirty seconds," the producer warned, so everyone settled down and made a good show of looking distracted by their phone screens. He held his hand up and then pointed in Vee's direction.

"Hey, hey, my entertainment peeps. Have I got a delicious treat for you today!" Her voice reached that exaggerated pitch again, but settled down a bit when she launched into a rapid-fire pace of questions.

Max let out the breath he was holding when she raved about his performance at the awards show and then asking about the band's latest music video.

"Oh, I'm stoked about that one. It's filmed on the lake back home." Max's smile was finally genuine.

"Ah yeah. The trailer park where you guys grew up. That's awesome letting us have a look into your underprivileged past."

With another reporter, one that didn't make their living gossiping, Max would have no worries talking about that part of him, but with Vee, he knew it was time to shut it down.

He opened his mouth, but she plowed on with another question.

"Tell me something I don't already know about the dynamics of this rags-to-riches band." She leaned forward, allowing too much cleavage on display.

Max knew it was her ploy to get him distracted into saying something he shouldn't. He'd been meandering through the entertainment life long enough to know most of the tricks of the trade. He averted his eyes to the camera and smirked while strumming a quick riff before moving his gaze to the mole peeking out of the makeup on her forehead.

"Sweet thang," he began, wanting to reel her in before launching down the music road. "You wanna know how we pulled this off?" He waved around the *grey* green room as though it were the accomplishment.

"Absolutely!" Vee leaned closer, her boobs dangerously teetering on the edge of full calamity right before the camera. Max locked his eyes above her nose just in case.

"I'm lead guitarist, but where most bands get a song going with the guitar, we put that in Mave's hands with the drums. Dude sets the beat, and then I ease in a sexy riff to draw in the crowd. Dillon is our rhythm guitarist. My man is the driving force, so it's fitting. Logan keeps us mellow with his bass and Trace tightens our sound with his keys. Now we got Will, and that fella can handle wherever we put him. It's epic."

Vee's eyes glazed over, but Max couldn't care less.

"I like my role in the band. It's the *only* thing I take seriously." He grinned, about to head down a silly path in true Maxim fashion, but Vee latched on to his last sentence like a crazed kitten clawing the catnip toy.

"Don't you take your *fiancée* seriously?"

The grin froze in awkward place. He cleared his throat and let out a nervous chuckle.

Her snarky eyes narrowed when she caught on to his hesitation. "Seems the two of you hardly spend any time together these days."

His shoulder shrugged before he could

stop the anxious gesture, but he somehow managed to keep eye contact with the reporter. He knew looking away would be a dead giveaway. "It's expected with our professions."

"Yes, but before your reconciliation with your estranged father last year, you and Mona were inseparable."

Max inwardly groaned. Nothing about last year's diabolical bombshell was reconciled. If anything, it had festered until the entire situation became way too sore to touch. Their father had shown up out of nowhere, begging the twin's mom to take him back. Thankfully, she had enough sense to decline, but she did feel sorry for her ex-husband for some reason Max couldn't comprehend. If it weren't for his mother, Max would have never agreed to meet him and then pay for the stranger's rehab expenses.

Before Max could conjure up an answer or figure out how to disappear instantly, his hat was snatched off his head. Looking around, he saw Dillon standing behind him holding it up high.

"Dude!" he yelled, standing up and trying to grab it back with one hand while covering his unkempt hair with the other.

With a devious grin and flick of his wrist,

Dillon sent the hat flying in Logan's direction. Max took off after it, easily giving Dillon the chance to plant himself in front of the camera.

"Sorry about that, sweetheart. Max had it coming. You know that punk dyed all my shirts pink! He deserved a bad hair day shot over that." He let out a deep chuckle while smoothing his hand down the front of his splotchy pink tee.

Dillon had been wearing the shirts without acknowledging anything obscure about them, not giving Max the satisfaction of his prank.

"Oh, I love those crazy tricks he likes to pull," she cooed, leaning forward again while batting her false eyelashes.

"Hate to cut this short, but we gotta kick it soon. Your pretty little self understands, right?"

"I…" Vee scrambled, trying to regain control of the interview, but Dillon wasn't having it.

"Here. Let me give you a custom Max shirt." Dillon grabbed the back of the pink tee and whipped it over his head in one fluid motion.

Vee's gasp of appreciation was quite loud as she gawked at Dillon's bare torso. The California sun had darkened his already bronze skin even further, showcasing his well-defined chest and abs. As though Blake read his mind, the perceptive assistant handed over a black Sharpie. Dillon scribbled his name across the front of the shirt before draping it over the reporters crossed legs.

"But…" Vee seemed unable to speak, her eyes glued to the stunning male physique on display right before her and the camera.

Dillon allowed a sultry smile to deepen the dimples in his cheeks. Offering the stunned reporter a wink, he tilted his head toward the door before leading his bandmates out of it.

Halfway down the hall, the group erupted in a roar of laughter.

"Bro, Jewels is gonna kick your butt for that stunt." Trace shook his head.

"Pretty Girl will understand I did what I had to do to rescue this punk." Dillon elbowed Max playfully.

They hustled into the dressing room, and as soon as the door shut, Max seemed to deflate into the couch. The mood instantly shifted to dark.

"You okay?" Dillon asked as he fastened the buttons of his indigo shirt Blake had just handed him.

Max hitched his shoulder. "Might as well

be. Thanks, man, for getting me outta there."

Dillon worked on rolling the sleeves up to his elbows. "You up for tonight?"

Shoulder shrug. "Sure."

"If you're not—" Ben chimed in, running his hand through his greying hair.

"No worries." Max stood abruptly, feeling the walls closing in on him. "I'll see y'all out there."

"Whoa there, speedy. Let's pray before you run off," Dillon said.

After the first amen was out, so was Max. He ambled around backstage, looking for a way to relieve some tension while dodging around stacks of black equipment trunks. A rush of chaos came near him, revealing the vile Vee and her crew being escorted by security.

"What's up?" he asked one of the security guards.

"Found them filming in a restricted area," the big guy answered, coming to a halt in front of Max.

He directed his attention to Vee, who was red-faced. "Ah now, sweet thang, you know better than that." Max winked as he shoved his hands into his front pockets, finding a tube of hand sanitizer he had especially prepared for Trace.

"Max, tell them it's okay. You *owe* me for blowing off the interview," Vee whined in that shrilling tone, sealing her fate.

"Vee, did you wash your hands since the interview?" Max asked, his fingers edging the tube out of his pocket.

She gave him a confused look before muttering, "No." She bolstered more attitude in the one little word than was necessary, in Max's opinion.

"Not good." His concerning voice and slow shake of his head belied the mischievous twinkle in his brown eyes. "Just found out a few of our assistants have suddenly come down with a nasty stomach bug."

Vee's attitude withered, her eyes widening. A well-known fact about Vee Declan was that she was an overly dramatic germaphobe. "How bad is it?"

"Both ends kind of *bad*." Max widened his eyes to match hers. "Here, I've got some hand sanitizer."

The words barely finished escaping his mouth as her hand reached out to swipe the little tube, squirting half of the contents out into her shaky palm before handing it back to him.

"It's quite thick," she mumbled while

trying to work the substance along the front and back of her hands.

"Yeah. Some new formula." His lip twitched with the lie, but Max was able to tamp down the grin. He nodded his head to the security guard and began walking away.

"My… my hands are stuck together! Maxim King!"

He heard her hissy fit but pretended otherwise. Trace met up with him in the corridor.

"What's Vee yelling about now?" Trace glared over Max's shoulder where she held her entwined hands up before disappearing from their view.

"Vee's just being Vee." Max dismissed that while pulling the tube back out of his pocket. "Say, Trace, did you know hand sanitizer looks a lot like that clear craft glue Grace and Phoebe were using this morning?"

"No…" Trace eyed the tube.

"Want some?" Max offered it over.

"Sure." Trace held his palm up to accept a generous squirt, totally clueless to Max's glue statement. "It's sticky."

"You make my job too easy, Space Cadet." With a deep laugh, feeling more like himself, Max hurried off before Trace could get his glue-coated hands around his pranking neck.

• ♫ • ♫ • ♫ •

The electric energy of the concert ricocheted around the dark corridors of backstage as people finally began heading out. The show went off in blazing success, but the bandmates kept a close eye on their lead guitarist. Everyone reaches a limit, and it was evident that he was nearing his.

The meet-and-greet with select fans finally wrapped around midnight. Max flexed his aching fingers as he headed out of the green room with Mave hot on his heels. His brother's hand clamped down on his shoulder before Max could make a clean break for it.

"Dude, I think it's time we paid dear ole Dad a visit." Mave regarded him with tense, brown eyes—identical to his own.

"I ain't got a dad."

"Maybe so, and now you ain't got a fiancée anymore either. What gives with that? The public is catching on." Mave crossed his heavily tattooed arms.

Before Max could mutter something to pacify his twin, Izzy came shuffling over with her face as red as...

"Hey, red hot chili pepper," Max teased, intensifying the hue of her flushed cheeks.

Mave looked over and reached for his shaken wife. "What's wrong?"

Her eyes darted between the twins. "Umm… I just… I just walked in on Will—"

Max barked in laughter. "You see our boy naked?"

Both Izzy and Mave shot him a warning scowl. He held his hands up in defense.

"No!" she whispered harshly while looking around. "He's in Dillon's dressing room, making out with Stella."

"Leona's assistant?" Max asked.

"Yes…" Izzy cleared her throat, waiting for a few stragglers to make it out the back exit. "They didn't see me, so I'm pretty sure they're still going at it."

Both twins grinned wickedly at each other as Mave reached for Izzy's hand. "Come on. Let's go bust up Casanova's party."

Sure enough, they found Will kissing the young woman passionately while she sat on top of the counter. His hands were grasping Stella's thin shoulders, close to pinning her against the mirror.

"Dude, you're doing it all wrong," Mave said loudly, making Will jump back. The eighteen-year-old's face was as flushed as Izzy's, but obviously for another reason entirely.

Stella wasted no time hopping down and hiding behind Will's broad back.

"Dude," was all he could get his husky voice to produce.

"Sweetheart, you never let some idiot manhandle you like that." Mave addressed her even though she was completely hidden from his view behind the giant teenage idiot. He quirked an eyebrow at said giant. "You gotta do better than that. You don't grip a girl like you're holding her prisoner."

Max wisely kept mute, knowing his name and eloquence did not go together whatsoever. He also knew he failed the subject on how to treat a lady. He merely offered an occasional nod in agreement with his brother and kept his mouth firmly shut.

"Watch and learn, punk," Mave said to Will as he offered his hand to Izzy, allowing her the choice to agree or not. When she placed her tiny palm into his, he gently pulled her close. "Hold her hand and take a moment to appreciate she trusts you enough to let you hold it." His eyes remained bonded to Izzy's as he spoke his lesson to Will. He then worked his other hand through her pale hair until it was cradling the back of her head while sliding their entwined fingers to her waist. Nothing was urgent or demanding with his touch. "You hold her in your arms as though the dream of this angel is too fragile and you absolutely fear her love will shatter." Mave paused to look over at Will. "'Cause, dude, she's *perfect* and you just can't chance losing this gift." Reverence laced each of his words.

Izzy squirmed slightly in his arms, uncomfortable from the attention. "Maverick," she murmured, meaning his name as a warning yet it came out more of a soft moan.

Mave leaned down until his lips were so close to his wife's that her heated breath warmed his skin, but he paused to allow her the respect of closing the small space between their lips. When she did, he led the kiss in the most delicate display of love Max had ever witnessed. It truly looked as though the drummer was terrified their bond would shatter if he was too aggressive. The moment was much more intimate than the full-blown make-out session they had interrupted.

When Mave stepped back, Izzy's face was back to scarlet. He winked at her before asking, "Do you mind escorting Stella out to the limo?"

"Okay." Her brown eyes held a dazed effect.

"Thanks, Doll. We'll be along shortly." He leaned down and brushed a parting kiss to her rosy lips.

Stella stepped around Will and followed Izzy out while keeping her gaze locked on the floor, her own cheeks slightly pink.

As soon as they were gone, Max turned his attention back to Will. "Man, you know better than that."

Will's arms shot up. "What's wrong with kissing a girl?"

"Nothing if you do it right," Mave shot back.

"We were just keyed up from the concert…" The young guy threaded his fingers through the top of his hair.

"I totally get ya about the performance high. So much adrenaline rushing through you it demands to be released, but you don't go taking it out on a girl like that," Mave continued his lecture as he propped up on the arm of the couch.

"Well, it sure felt good."

"To who?" Max added, eyeing the flustered kid with skepticism.

"Me." Will offered a cocky smirk with both twins responding with stern frowns.

"And that's where you're wrong again, and being disrespectful. You always pay attention to your lady's needs, not your own. You are to make her feel special and cherished, not used like you just did to Stella."

"If your old man had seen that, he would have knocked you upside the head," Max muttered.

Mave moved the conversation bluntly to the heart of the matter to set the hormone-crazed guy straight. "Best advice is to keep it in your pants until you make a commitment." Mave held his hand up to emphasize his point with the silver wedding band adorning his finger.

"That's why you married Izzy not even two months after y'all met," Will accused, crossing his arms.

"No, you idiot. God granted me a gift that I wasn't even worthy to have. No way was I not accepting it as fast as I could."

Max stepped over to Will and rested his hand on his young buddy's shoulder. "Seriously, hold on to that gift until you're married. Don't waste it on stupid hormones."

Will glanced between the brothers. "Did

you guys waste it?"

The twins exchanged a look. Max nodded his head before answering. "Some of us, but your mom and dad didn't waste it. They waited to share that gift until they were married. Those two are the example you need to follow. The love they have is epic, and totally what God intended it to be."

Mave finally smiled and eased the conversation into concluding on a lighter note. "But, dude, don't forget there's nothing wrong with flirting and showing a chick you're interested. Just keep in mind to never disrespect her."

"Alright. I got ya." Will rushed out the door to get away from the uncomfortable lecture, unaware of the presence in the dark hall.

The twins left out after him, but halted when they detected the hallway wasn't empty. They were used to keeping aware of their surroundings, another lesson Will needed to be schooled on.

"You coulda went in there and helped us set your kid straight," Max grumbled.

Dillon pushed off the wall and handed both guys a greasy bag filled with burgers and fries. The savory scent of their late-night snack filled the space, making them groan. Both were shoveling fat fries into their mouths before Dillon could speak.

"Sounded like the two of you had it under control."

Max looked up sheepishly, cheeks poking out from the huge bite of burger he'd just taken. "I'm not sure if we are the best choice for the birds-and-bees kinda talks," he muffled out between chews.

"You forget too quickly how I screwed up my first kiss with Jewels. I stole it, remember?" Dillon confessed. He and Mave shared a chuckle as they made their exit, but Max was stone-cold serious.

With the day he had just endured—or week or month or year for that matter—he knew he was nowhere close to being the man God intended him to be. The harsh evidence nudged him. An unforgiving and sometimes spiteful heart. Less than honest lips. Selfishly withdrawing from loved ones. Many twisted mistakes had the greasy food churning in his gut by the time they joined the others in the back of the limo.

Handing Mave his half-eaten bag of food, Max closed his eyes and could only see the blaring failure of not being the Godly man he was supposed to be to Mona. She was a gift and he did nothing but take it for granted, misusing her trust along the way, and then disposing her love like it was nothing more than garbage.

The lump in his throat increased as the vice grip of shame clamped against him as he realized he was no better than his estranged father. Treating people with blatant disregard and then abandoning them when his own demons became too much to bear.

Everyone continued the celebration well into the night. Except for Max. He disappeared into his room soon after they returned to the beach house. The night was long with sleep evading the guilt-stricken guitarist. He'd begun to think life was too long in general.

SIX

"Ride"
-twenty one pilots

One thing is for certain—life can be one tricky son-of-a-gun. It can cause even the wisest individual a false sense of comfort, eluding one into thinking everything is under control.

Maybe not completely under control, but manageable.

And then, within a blink, a circumstance can snatch the rug right out from under the poor idiot's feet. Oh, but it most certainly can get worse if that individual doesn't open those blinded eyes fast enough. Life can go down a long, long, path of self-doubt, self-pity, and self-destruction.

Maxim King was being taken for such a ride by his own circumstances, but seemed to be in no hurry of slamming on the brakes. He sat on the edge of his bed in a familiar room that had become unfamiliar overnight. Gone were the deep-blue walls that had always reminded him of his sapphire Fender. Now an odd hue of mint-green engulfed him, reminiscent of the toothpaste he favored.

"Ain't feeling it on the walls though," Max muttered to himself, while inspecting the renovated space. It had become too light and airy for his ever-present dark mood as of late.

Leona used sea life as the design inspiration for the beach house. Each room was dressed hues of blues and greens and corals with accents of soft greys.

"You ready?" Mave interrupted.

"Might as well be." With a sigh of resignation, Max stood while pulling on the ball cap he had clutched in his hand and headed out.

"No need in worrying. All's gonna be fine." Mave slapped him on the back forcefully as they eased into the back of the SUV.

Max wanted to tell Mave it was easy for him to say don't worry when it wasn't him in the hot seat, but kept his mouth shut for a change.

"Yo, Sonny. What's happening?" Max leaned up and shook their driver's hand.

"Ah, nothin' but driving you spoiled brats around." His dark face beamed in amusement. Ben wouldn't allow them out the door unless they agreed to let their bodyguard drive them. They had kept it between just the band about the appointment, and Max had to talk stern to make the rest of the guys stay behind. He saw no reason in needing five of them to hold his grown hand.

"Walker just wanted you to take precautions. You probably just need a worm treatment." Mave chuckled at his own joke as he settled in beside Max. He tried conveying a light demeanor, but the anxious drumbeat he tapped against his knee was a dead giveaway to his worry.

Max's trainer showed up last week as he did every week since the group had arrived in California to put the guitarist through a rigorous weight training workout. Walker jotted down Max's food intake for the prior week during his warmup, which confessed to the twenty hot dogs he ate during a challenge with Mave where Mave ended up in the same condition as Will. Entire pizzas, pies, cakes, huge steak dinners, dozens of burgers, large quantities of chicken and waffles, some fruits and vegetables, and three daily protein shakes rounded out the food journal. By the time Walker finished recording the atrocious list, his brows were pinched heavily with concern.

"It's time we get you checked out. Something's off." Those hesitant words from Walker were the reason Max was on his way to the hospital for bloodwork.

"Maybe you have a hormonal imbalance. That would explain your mood swings..." Mave kept rambling off cheesy comments while Max remained mute until they arrived.

The guys were able to enter the hospital without a flurry of attention for a change, helping Max's frazzled nerves settle a bit. The entire exam and bloodwork took very little time with the staff already prepared to accommodate the rocker as quickly and quietly as possible. Hidden away in a back office, the clock slowed to a hesitant tick while they waited for the results. Thankfully, Sonny brought in an Italian pasta feast since Max had to fast for the tests. The three guys ate with gusto, but remained relatively quiet.

A light tap on the door sounded as a

doctor with Asian descent walked in with a folder tucked under his arm.

"Mr. King, it's a pleasure to meet you." He shook Max's hand and then offered it to Mave. "As well as you, Mr. King." *Clearly a fan.*

"Thanks, Dr. Cheng," Max replied, reading the name stitched on the white lab coat.

"Just call me Nori." He plopped in a chair and pulled on a pair of thick-framed glasses. Opening the file, he began reviewing the test results.

"He's got worms, right?" Mave spoke, causing the doctor to look up from the chart.

Max leveled his smart-aleck brother with a warning look.

"No parasites were found," the doctor answered seriously, not realizing the joke. "However, the numbers on your thyroid are abnormal. Since this seems to be something that's been going on for quite a while, I'd like to run a few more tests."

With that, the afternoon droned by with a battery of tests that were eventually explained to the confused man and his brother.

"Hyperthyroidism is a condition where the thyroid produces too much thyroid hormone. That explains why Max can eat with no weight gain and also why he always feels starved," the doctor said as he scribbled on a prescription pad. "Anxiety and irritability are also symptoms."

This comment elicited a grunt and an exaggerated nod from Mave. Those were recent symptoms, and Max knew his thyroid wasn't the cause, but he kept quiet with only offering a shoulder shrug and nod of confirmation.

After the doctor handed over a few prescriptions and Mave lined up tickets for their next concert to be delivered to Dr. Cheng, the guys finally headed out.

The whirling sound of the automated doors preceded the tinkering clicks of multiple cameras directed at the twins. The flickering of flashes and shouts from the paparazzi had Mave stepping ahead of Max as the two of them hurried toward the SUV. They ignored the shouts of rude questions and dove into the backseat.

"Well, at least things should straighten out now that we know what's ailing ya." Mave began tapping a beat against the leather seats while looking relieved.

He should have known better.

● ♫ ● ♫ ● ♫ ●

One day… One trip to the hospital… And one unfortunate picture. That's all it took to turn the gossip rags into a tizzy of bogus reports that spread quicker than an irritated rash.

As Max flipped through the latest gossip magazine, his thoughts pondered about how a celebrity could be painted in a glamourous Godlike depiction in one moment, but then completely shrouded in condemnation and vulgarity the next.

The pictures and the false headlines proved it. *Rock Nation's Drummer King Falls, Maverick Takes a Tumble, Rehab for the Rocker.* The lie was even trending on the social media sites.

"This is stupid!" Max roared as he slung the magazine across the kitchen, landing it in the trash where it rightfully belonged. "Dude is clean."

"We know that, and more importantly, God knows." Tate clamped Max on the shoulder for reassurance, but it did little good.

His phone vibrated with an incoming text. Max pulled it out of his pocket and stomped to the back. Relief flooded his system at the sight of Mona's name on the phone screen, even though he knew he wasn't worthy of it.

Mona – *R u ok?*

The media took the pictures of the twins leaving the hospital as a sign that Mave was the one in duress, but Mona knew them well enough to pick up on the fact that in every photo Mave stood in front of his brother as a shield for him. It was an instinctual habit the twins shared.

Max inhaled a shaky breath and typed a reply. *Good news, I don't have worms. Bad news, stupid thyroid is jacked up.* He hit send and sank into a lounge chair.

Mona – *That doesn't sound good to me.*

Max – *No worries. Nothing a pill won't fix.* He hit send, but cringed when rereading it, so he sent another one. *Need to get the heat off Mave. Will u release a statement about me having hyperthyroid and being treated.* His fingers faltered a beat with knowing that wouldn't be enough juice to sate the media, so he added, *also let them in on our split.*

A long pause punctuated her hurt before Mona replied with a simple, *ok.*

Nausea rolled through his gut with knowing he was intentionally inflicting pain on Mona, as well as himself, in order to save his brother from the lynch mob.

"Are you alright?" Jewels asked as she sat on the end of the lounge chair and nudged his leg.

"Right as rain."

Jewels shook her head. "You don't fool me, Maxim King." She reached over and boldly read the texts still on the screen.

"Nosy much?" He yanked the phone away and shoved it in his pocket.

"What happened with Mona?"

"She deserved better."

"Is that what she said?" A slice of irritation mingled with her tone.

"I said," he quietly answered, hoping to hush the topic away.

"Oh please. How lame is that?"

"How many years did you hold on to the same notion you weren't good for Dillon? Half your life at least. Yeah, how lame?" Sarcasm deepened his voice.

Jewels was undeterred by his jab, waving her hand as though dismissing her own foolishness into the ocean breeze. "You can use my lame excuse all you want, but you still don't fool me. You've gotten this bizarre idea stuck in your hardhead that if you abandon them first, then they won't have the chance to do it to you."

"Now you sound like Aunt Evie." Max snorted, pushing a teasing elbow into her side as he sat up.

"Why thank you." Jewels quietly giggled before growing somber. "But you really opened your life to Mona. It was the first time you've allowed it with a woman. I don't understand." Her green eyes softened with sympathy.

"I tried, Jewels, but I ended up doing what I always do. I did manage to open the door, but when junk got real I found another exit and pushed her out of it." A harsh huff trembled out of him. "Man, I'm messed up."

"You need to knock it off, and let someone in permanently. I had really hoped Mona was going to be the one—"

"She deserves better than having to deal with my issues."

"More like stupidities." Jewels leaned forward, demanding the attention he had averted toward the deck. She stopped holding her tongue long ago, not babying them over important issues at the expense of hurting their feelings.

"Whatever, Jewels. I need to go check on my brother." Max pushed to his feet, hoping the pressure building in his chest would alleviate.

"He asked Izzy to give him some space." She followed close behind him to the glass doors, allowing him to run away from the subject for the time being.

"And she actually listened?"

"Yeah. Poor guy. Those dumb reports dredged up some harsh memories. He looked right sick."

Max ran his fingertips through the thick scruff on his chin. "I'll fix it," he muttered, closing the back door and making a beeline right out the front one.

Two hours later he was back with several boxes of fried goodness and two gallons of milk. That part only took a smidgen of the time he was gone. The rest of it was successfully spent with him hanging out with paparazzi, filling them in on his thyroid issue and even allowing them to film him jamming out in a local pawnshop's music section. The owner wasn't thrilled with the commotion at first, until realizing who the mischievous customer was. Before Max made it too far into the show word broke about Mona and his split, so he took time to help spread that around also, tolerating several rounds of Q & A's with the weasels following him around.

Did you cheat?

No, dude. You don't cheat on babes like Mona Fielding.

Did she cheat?

I wouldn't blame her, but no. Mona is a saint.

Are you seeing anyone?

No.

What's up with your brother?

Nothing, he's standing by me while I deal with my health and breakup. Dude is awesome like that. He's a saint, too.

He allowed them answers they had no right to know, all to set things straight about his brother. His skin ached as though the pain of exposing himself so openly were causing his pores to bleed acid, but his lazy smile never faltered.

Not until he pushed into his brother's bedroom.

In that moment, everything faltered and flashed him right back to being nine years old. The luscious aroma of cinnamon and vanilla vanished along with the vast beach house suite, regressing to the tiny trailer reeking of musty disappointment. The large lump of man under the expensive comforter transformed into a barely noticeable bump under the threadbare quilt of the double bed.

"Whatcha doin'?" Max stood at the end of their shared bed.

"Hiding." Mave's voice muffled out through his fabric fortress.

"From what?"

"Everything."

Max's small shoulder hitched up in a halfhearted shrug. "Aunt Evie done said you can't hide from God."

"Well, I ain't speaking to God right now."

"Why not?"

"'Cause he didn't make Daddy stay."

Once Mave mumbled that, Max just wanted to hide, too. Their dad had hightailed it that morning, saying he couldn't do the family thing anymore, leaving them confused and inconsolable.

Max and his wounded heart climbed under the cover with his brother, not acknowledging the tears streaming from the corners of Mave's eyes. After settling underneath the quilt, he offered the only comfort afforded at the time—half of a melting candy bar he snuck from Aunt Evie's trailer earlier that day. It was the place he ran off to when his wasted father told him to get lost before peeling out of the trailer park in the late model El Camino, which left them vehicle-less. The boys remained hidden, listening to their mom quietly sobbing in her tiny room beside them until their bellies *demanded they find something else to fill the harsh void.*

Thankfully they chose food to fill it for most of their lives. That was until Mave tried unsuccessfully to fill it with drugs.

Max wished he were wise enough back then to understand for them both that there was no hiding from the disappointment of reality. Nor could that void of abandonment be filled with anything worldly, because nothing ever sated that pain for very long.

He shook the memory off, knowing that particular bruise needed no pressure added to its already throbbing state, and yanked the blanket back so he could climb in, too.

"It's not a candy bar, but I figured four dozen gourmet donuts will do us better."

Mave cracked his eyes open to confirm his brother had the goods. "Yeah, they'll do in a pinch," he agreed in a gruff voice.

Both guys settled against the whitewashed headboard as Max handed over two boxes and a gallon of milk. He knew this was still not dealing with reality, but filling the void with a temporary fix.

At least it's not the drugs he's being accused of, Max thought as he stole a glance at his disheveled twin still in his pajama bottoms and wrinkled tee at two in the afternoon.

"Dang," Mave muttered, inhaling the divine aroma released as he peeled open the lid of the white box. "Apple fritters."

"Straight up," Max agreed, shoving half of one in his mouth.

Smacking and groans filled the quiet space until they both had a dozen treats polished off.

"So Leona gave y'all a pink room." Max quirked an eyebrow at his twin.

"It's *coral*," Mave drawled, clearly mocking Leona.

They both took in the newly designed room with the muted coral walls, white furniture, and pewter accents.

"What's the difference?" Max's shoulder hitched up.

"Exactly."

Before they could continue averting their attention from the true problem at hand, Izzy's blonde head appeared through the slightly opened door. Her brown eyes searched over her husband before focusing on Max.

"That was very generous of you, Max." She eased over to the edge of the bed and swiped a fritter from Mave's second box.

"No doubt. It wasn't easy sharing these babies." He held a donut up in salute before taking a substantial bite out of it.

Izzy pulled her phone out and handed it over to Mave as evidence. "You know what I'm talking about."

"Dude, you didn't have to air your relationship laundry like that." Mave showed him the social media headline. *M&M Breakup*. It was the couple's nickname dubbed by the entertainment world.

"It was my fault they attacked you in the first place." He focused on polishing off the fritter, not wanting to talk about it anymore.

Izzy leaned over and placed a soft kiss on his bearded cheek. "Thank you for clearing up that mess for my man."

He looked at her a bit surprised. Izzy was never one to offer him any affection beings they had a love/hate relationship reminiscent of feuding siblings.

"Yeah, thanks for that." Mave pushed his shoulder against Max's before it could shrug off the accolades.

"Ain't my niceness worth at least barbeque chicken and tater salad?" He waggled his eyebrows in Izzy's direction, playing down the weightiness.

"Yes, I totally agree." She grinned.

"Without any peppers, right?" Max looked

at her hopeful, eliciting the desired laugh from his brother.

"It just so happens I'm clean out of peppers at the moment."

"Awesome. You best be on with it then, woman, 'cause we're 'bout done with our appetizers." Max pointed to the second box that was already half empty before trying to shoo her away.

Izzy popped him playfully. "You better watch your attitude, Pepper Man." She made for the door, clearly on a barbeque mission.

"Hey, Doll. You forgot something." Mave said, causing her to backtrack as though her body was tethered to his possessive tone.

She leaned down, her lips a breath from his. "I could never forget you." She planted a kiss on him that made even Max blush.

"Good grief. Warn a man next time so I can bolt." Max's grouchy voice was a mix of truth and tease.

"Don't be jealous," Izzy sassed as she nearly skipped out the door.

The guys went back to devouring the fritters in silence. Mave was clearly thinking about that kiss from his Doll Baby with a faint smile lifting the corners of his lips. Max's own thoughts were a million miles in the past, his brows pinched and the sweet treat turning a bit sour on his tongue.

I could never forget you...

Those words played on repeat through his mind, but they were not in Izzy's singsong voice. They echoed from his own voice, cocky and so sure of himself. Then the echo transformed into a rusty version that was weak from alcohol abuse.

I could never forget you, babe...

Max was so sure he had life figured out when he declared that to Mona. It was moving smoothly in a direction most promising.

I could never forget you, son...

But his father did forget. Martin King resurfaced and ruined the smooth ride, causing Max's life to veer off course before completely crashing.

Some ride...

SEVEN

"How Will I Know"
-Lydia Laird

Sunshine caressed the lake, striking the water ablaze in millions of facets, mesmerizing and magical. The acoustic guitar softly played the enchanting scene its love song with the guitarist mimicking the subtle flow of the lake from the chords strummed.

Her body was positioned between him and the guitar, not only wanting to hear the lullaby better but to also feel its power reverberate through her body. Mona was born with partial hearing loss, but was in love with music more than anyone Max had ever met. It seemed her impairment drove her to appreciate sounds more so than someone who took their gift of full hearing for granted. He hardly believed it when they met, thinking it was a part of the PR firm's ploy to sign the band. He held on to his leeriness for nearly a year before he let it go. Mona was a person that not only listened and appreciated music, but also thoroughly experienced it with her body and soul. No doubt, Max fell hard.

With the pale sand tickling his toes and the warmth of the sun and Mona's body pressing against him, Max could think of nowhere else he'd rather be than on the tiny, secluded beach behind his lakefront cabin at Shimmer Lakes. He was home where he belonged. As his nimble fingers continued to draw music from his beloved guitar, Max whispered a prayer of thanksgiving.

"Thank you for this glimpse of heaven," he began with eyes sweeping the lake scene painted in God's splendor, "and thank you for the angel in my arms." No one had ever fit his embrace so perfectly.

"What was that?" Mona tilted her good ear toward his mouth.

Max took advantage and slowly nipped his teeth against the delicate flesh along the shell of her ear, eliciting a vibration to shimmy along her body and on through his.

"Just thanking the Man for my life," he whispered before pressing a kiss behind her ear and continuing down her neck.

"The Man probably doesn't think highly of you taking advantage of the side of my neck." Mona gasped out a giggle when his teeth grazed her sensitive skin.

"Nah, sweetness. God's the creator of love. This is just me expressing it to my fiancée," he proudly stated, taking a moment to appreciate the extravagant ring glittering in the sun. "You should have agreed to Vegas, so I could be expressing it completely."

She giggled again. The day he presented the engagement ring, Max had also proposed they should immediately hop on a private jet to Vegas. Mona accepted the ring, but declined the rushed nuptials.

"You know I'm not one to rush into things."

Max smiled at the memory while he continued to strum lazily. She looked up with her light-teal eyes holding so much love, he couldn't help but steal a kiss.

"I cannot get over how you play the guitar without focusing on it at all," she said against his lips.

He had, in fact, been playing continuously during the entire span of the conversation and caresses without missing one chord, effortlessly flowing one song into the next.

"Music is a part of me. There's no forgetting it's there. It just is. The most steady part of my life, that music." He nodded his head to the guitar he continued to strum.

"I'm always here." Mona's words slipped quietly, but Max felt the loudness of them.

"And I could never forget you, babe." He dropped the guitar beside him, so he could hold onto his promise to her. Wrapping his arms tightly around the angel, he kissed her until the bruises of his heart were subdued.

The life he dreamt for Mona and himself was as smooth and exquisite as the lake in front of them. Never did he see a storm from his past lurking to throw him so far off course that he lost what he promised to never forget.

It took a year after that spring day by the lake to plan out the wedding, and it took one phone call to cancel it all out.

• ♫ • ♫ • ♫ •

Max stood like stone beside his mother and

twin as they checked the man who had abandoned the three of them decades ago into a rehab, promising to be there for him after he failed to do that himself.

A tall yet considerably frail man who barely resembled the man his nine-year-old eyes remembered. *Was that just a delusion of my memory*, Max had questioned many times after that day at the facility in Atlanta. The very same place Dillon had helped him check Mave into after the drummer survived an overdose.

The beat being tapped along his thigh was rather aggressive as Mave kept his eyes trained on the floor. No doubt, reminiscing with his painful past. Max and his mom offered to handle the paperwork without him, but Mave wouldn't allow them to go through the difficult task without him.

Martin King sat slumped in a chair in the corner of the admittance office, sallow complexion and the noticeable shake of withdrawals. Max could barely stomach to look at him, yet curiously couldn't look away. Martin's hazel eyes, bloodshot and glassy from crying, kept meeting his but would dart away quickly.

After they had Martin settled into his room, he began with the too-late apologies.

"Just save it, will ya. Just... Just focus on getting yourself better." Max shook his head in disgust at the poor excuse for a father.

Martin ran his trembling hand through the sparse brown hair on top of his head, in a state of confusion. "I never forgot about you."

"You did the moment you walked out the door," Max snapped, his temper barely restrained. All of the hurt, anger, and disappointment began a rapid boil, close to spewing all over the place.

He turned to escape it, but his estranged father's hand lunged out to halt the progress. "Please, Maxim. I made an awful mess, but you gotta understand I could never forget you, son."

Max had no desire to repeat himself, knowing the alcohol had damaged the eldest King's mind to the point of no repair. Yanking out of Martin's frail grasp, Max locked his jaw to prevent his words from coming out in a shout. "You got what you wanted. The bill is paid up, so there's no need for this act."

Mave followed Max out and both never looked back. The only interaction they had in Martin's life after that day was to pay for hospital stays or when another rehab visit needed paying.

One day was all it took to put things back into blaring perspective. Max walked away that day feeling all of nine years old again, abandoned and not good enough to keep. A month of fixating on the past had planted enough doubt and distrust for Max to effectively push Mona away. He wouldn't give her the opportunity to abandon him as well.

His life had been one raucous circus filled with pranks and silly flings before Mona. He didn't do serious or stable. Max only did fun and fleeting and he thought it was time for him to get back to it when he sat her down to have a talk.

"This ain't gonna happen, babe. I'm sorry. You deserve better. I hope you find much better, but I'll never forget you…"

EIGHT

"Father of Mine"
-Everclear

"Good Good Father"
-Chris Tomlin

"It's time to rock, suckers!" Will yelled as the band rushed the stage, the fans already hitting a crescendo of epic proportions. His guitar was slung over his shoulder, prepared to go toe to toe with Max from a fan's request earlier at the preshow meet-and-greet.

Ben had shrugged his shoulder in true Max fashion and said, "Why not," when the band eyed their designated daddy for permission.

Taking the stage, a weird vibe raced over Max and delivered icy prickles along his heated skin. He rolled his neck and shoulders to rid himself of the odd sensation, but it seemed to have taken root to stay. He stubbornly ignored it as he went into show-mode, grinning slyly at the crowd, focusing on the front row where he delivered a few winks to some of the cute chicks waving wildly at him. He even paused to touch some of the hands that were excitedly stretched toward him.

Will, wrapped in his blissful bubble, joined in the flirty display while following behind Max to center stage. Stagehands assisted them with getting the guitars plugged into the amps before disappearing. Without offering any discussion or welcome, the two launched right into a guitar showdown. Halfway through, Max halted his young friend's attempt to outplay him.

"Whoa, whoa, man. Didn't I teach you anything over the years? You gotta show the strings whose boss." Max's nimble fingers glided over the strings as though they were soft as feathers. "Maybe you should just go back to beating on drums with hotshot over there." He tilted his head in Mave's direction where the drummer was perched behind his drum kit.

The drums came to life in a killer performance with the crowd erupting in approval. Mave owned each beat in a dazzling show of dexterity, stealing the show.

Without warning, the strange sensation tapped Max on the shoulder and managed to snag his attention away from his brother. Glancing toward the audience, his mom caught his eye first, followed by a familiar figure beside her. There was no mistaking the thin shoulders or that Roman nose, matching closely to his own.

There sat Martin King in the audience, a scene Max had dreamt about so often over the years. To see his father witness the level of success he and his brother had achieved with no assistance from him at all. It should have been satisfying. It should have given him a vindicated feeling. Should have…

Fury rippled through Max like a deadly electrical current. The very sight of his father in the crowd, looking proud of all things, royally ticked the guitarist off. Martin's eyes locked with Max's, leading the elder King to smile and the younger King to glower. With bitterness turning his entire being sour, Max marched off the stage.

The pounding of his harsh pulse in his ears came close to blocking out the drum's solo. Taking several deep breaths, he slowly turned to watch the show, knowing he had to get himself in check in order to do his job.

Mave tossed his sticks into air with theatrical flair before holding them out to Will. "Looks like we need to show ole Max how it's done." The fans went into a tizzy as Mave relinquished his spot and headed off stage to his brother's side.

The drums came back to life. Will's mohawk was growing out, but he was somehow able to continue to style it in that fashion. His hair bobbed intensely back and forth in time with the rapid beats he elicited from the instrumental beasts before him.

"Man, you're playing the crowd tonight, and they're eating that junk up!" Mave slapped him five. His brown eyes were bright and sweat had begun to soak the collar of his dark tee.

"Yeah? You get a good look at that crowd tonight?" Max questioned skeptically, his eyes automatically traveled to that one irritating spot amongst the audience.

"Yeah! Packed out!" Mave's answer

confirmed that he had no idea their father was there.

"I'm feeling the need for some Everclear!" Max shouted over the roar of the fans as Will concluded his solo.

Mave bellowed out his own whoop for his protégé, before asking, "Which song?"

Max held back the wicked smile begging to come out and play, knowing he was about to gift their old man with some spitefulness due to him. "Father of Mine."

The song choice had Mave's head whipping in his twin's direction. "Dude, don't let him getting out of rehab get to ya. The story will die down in a day or two."

"You're a fine one to talk," Max grouched out, eyes narrowed. When Mave's light mood darkened, Max held his hands up with hopes of halting the progress. "Sorry. I just wanna blow off some steam. Ya feel me?"

Mave nodded before heading back out to the stage with Max slowly following.

"You two care to join this concert tonight?" Dillon ragged them, resulting in several catcalls from the audience.

Both twins chose to ignore the smart remark.

Mave leaned toward the mic Dillon held.

"How's about we give Ben a few more grey hairs tonight?"

Dillon's grin pulled until both dimples flashed deep in his scruffy cheeks. "Whattaya have in mind?"

Max answered in a hushed voice so the audience wouldn't hear, "Father of Mine."

Dillon's dimples fled, but Mave didn't give him a chance to decline by yanking the mic out of his massive grip.

"Anybody out there with *daddy issues* tonight?" The drummer growled into the mic, provoking the crowd to erupt. His free fist pumped in the air, joining in with those waving their hands while wailing out their own disappointments.

Dillon moved away while the ruckus escalated to let Trace and Logan in on the changeup tune of choice. He then positioned himself behind the drums with Will looking on with confused excitement from beside him.

The first chords of the song screeched from the electric guitar as Max played with more hostility than the opening merited. The other bandmates tried to bring their instruments to life to match his tone, each one losing themselves in the aggression.

"Father of ours, where have you been?" Mave

nearly screamed the lyrics while Max abused the guitar until one of the strings broke under the weight of his vehemence.

Mave sang about their world disappearing along with their dad. How their dad's wasted life didn't include them, and all he did was give them a name and then walked away.

Mave moved over to his brother, yelling his own version of the song, *"We were just nine-year-olds getting by the best we could. It wasn't easy for us being skinny boys in a poor neighborhood."* He moved the mic to share, so Max could join in shouting out the painful disappointment of their childhood.

"Our dad gave us a name... Daddy gave us a name... then he ran away!"

Mave took a step back to give the spotlight to Max as he took off into the guitar solo. The place erupted as he fell to his knees, agilely provoking the instrument to relent each chord in a devastating performance. Many eyes in the crowd released their own hurt, tears flowing in abandon.

Once Max pushed back to his feet, Mave draped his arm around his brother's shoulder and sang on, *"Now that I'm a grown man with two kids of my own, I promise I'll never let them know the pain I have known."*

They launched into the chorus, yelling the lyrics repeatedly with the band joining in. *"Our dad gave us a name... then he ran away!"*

Max allowed the sneering grin free as they concluded the song, giving a figurative finger to their estranged father. Mave pumped his fist in the air, but stuttered in his celebration. Max felt the pressure of his brother's glare before looking to confirm, knowing Mave had finally spotted Martin in the audience. His twin had hurts just as deep as his own, but chose to not allow their dad any glimpse his vulnerability. Singing that song had been a deliberate display of his insecurities without his permission.

"Not cool," Mave mouthed before heading back to his drums to trade spots with Dillon. They exchanged a few words before he sat down. His warm eyes had turned to ice as he kept slicing his brother steely glances.

Dillon swiftly marched over to Max while the arena broke out in a turbulent round of applause. He whispered sternly while holding the mic behind his broad back, "The man may have earned that, but didn't deserve it. I ain't putting up with us being disrespectful to anyone." He didn't wait for a reply before moving back to center stage, leaving Max feeling like the scolded brat he was.

After the fans finally settled down, Dillon addressed them, "Now these guys were just blowing off some steam." He shot Max a grin while shaking his head, obviously putting on a show for the crowd, but the depths of his dark-blue eyes didn't have Max fooled. "But can I be honest with y'all for a moment?" The fans clapped and whistled in agreement.

"Uh-oh. Here comes a lesson," Max muttered to himself as a stagehand traded out his electric guitar for an acoustic. He gave the guy a chin-jerk of thanks but kept his focus on the big dude at the front of the stage. There was a reason why Dillon Bleu was the leader of their group, and Max knew he was about to give a clear reminder as to why.

Dillon strummed over the strings of his own acoustic absently after another stagehand provided it to him. It became clear he was adding another changeup to the show, as he spoke, "Daddy issues, Momma issues, family issues, friend issues, even enemy issues... We all have them, because none of us are perfect. We all screw up and let our loved ones down at some point. Not saying it's cool, it's not, but we all make mistakes along this life's road." He played a hushed melody, allowing the band enough time to catch it and join in. "But we all have one Father, who is perfect and good and will never abandon us. That's what we need to focus on… Not what people have done wrong to us, but all the right God has done on our behalf."

And there it was, loud and clear, the lesson Max kept avoiding and ultimately failing to grasp. His focus had blurred away from God over the last few years, and selfishly fixated on the bitterness of the past. He could see nothing past the hazy residue left by his resentment toward his father, and honestly, toward his mother for allowing their dad to do it to them. Yes, that was the confused child lashing out against his mom over something she had no control over, but Max felt that way nonetheless.

Dillon began to croon the sincere lyrics of Chris Tomlin's "Good Good Father" as Max searched for Will, finding him standing toward the back of the stage. The song's message was about how perfect God is and how everyone is searching for answers only He can provide. The pressure swelled in Max's chest, but panic set in before he allowed his broken soul to come to terms with what God was whispering to him. He caught Will's attention and signaled the young guy to take his spot before slinking off the stage and right out the back exit, not stopping until he was as lost in the night as he was in his life.

NINE

"You and Your Heart"
-Jack Johnson

"Lullaby"
-Jack Johnson

"There was no call for that, young man." Judith King's sternness left no room for argument. Her dark hair whipped across her face from the sea breeze, obscuring her disappointment for a brief second before she swiped it behind her ear.

"Yes, ma'am," Max agreed, not wanting to disrespect his mother no more than he already had even though it was directed toward his estranged father. He angled his body in the lounge chair away from her, already burning from the scolding he'd been receiving for the last ten minutes straight.

A sniffle sounded from beside him, drawing Max's wandering attention that was close to zoning out over the surf, but he didn't acknowledge his mom's lamentation.

"Max, your father is dying." Her voice barely carried the news over the crashing waves.

He blinked the ocean away before giving her a sidelong glance. "What?" Max's heart wasn't of a cold variety. Sickness was something he would never wish on the puny man slumping in the deck chair across from him.

"Cirrhosis of the liver… Stage four." Judith choked on the last part, proving that somehow she still cared quite deeply for her ex. "He needs us." She reached out to touch Max's fisted hand, but he flinched away.

"Yeah?" His heart wasn't cold, but now on fire with rage. He focused his scrutiny to his father, but the man refused to look up. "Well, my brother already died once. Where was Martin when we needed *him*?"

That declaration caused a weathered set of

hazel eyes to finally snap up. "He died? You mean Mave?"

Max jabbed a finger toward the beach where his tatted-up brother was building a sandcastle with his own set of twins. Mave totally contradicted the bad-boy image he liked to play up for the fans. He may have owned that image earlier in his career, but he couldn't have been any farther away from it now.

"Yeah. *That* Mave. The almost-perfect match to me. That devoted dad on the beach sharing happy memories with his kids, not caring how goofy he looks in the process." Max took a shaky breath to calm the storm raging inside him. When he tried to speak again, his strong voice presented gravelly. "The guy over there didn't have any happy memories with his own dad, and went seeking that fulfillment in some dark places. Overdosed while trying to find it."

"Max," his mom whispered to soothe as well as hush him, but it went ignored.

"I was there when the medics couldn't find a pulse. It was me who watched on as they were close to pronouncing him dead." Max shook his head in disbelief as the nightmare of that night overwhelmed him—a medic pushing against Mave's silent heart to force it back to motion, another trying to breathe life back into his vacant body while another one glanced at his watch to call the time of death. "Me and Dillon… We did the only thing we could, crashing to our knees and begging God to give him a second chance while they worked on him. By nothing less than a miracle, God did."

"I'm sorry," Martin said, regret gripping both words.

The flames licking Max's battered heart escalated up to his eyes, but he refused to allow the tears to douse it. Sniffing them back vehemently, he rose from the lounge chair, feeling unsteady. Clutching his chest, he muttered, "I'm sorry, too, because both of our hearts were damaged by you. My brother's heart has healed, but mine is broke in a spot and I ain't able to figure out how to get it back together."

"Son, I know you're hurt, but this is about your dad's health crisis."

Max's eyes roamed back to his twin, wondering why he was getting a pass from that heavy conversation. Then something told him Mave already knew. "I'll pay whatever it costs to fix your liver. That's all I have to offer you." He hurried off the deck, fleeing the pain, since the tide refused to take it away as it receded.

Judith called out before the door shut all the way. "But there's no fixing it."

Max couldn't agree more. None of it was fixable. He kept on his path of escape, not slowing until he was hidden in the recesses of the first floor, where he found Will strumming the customized Gibson.

Will glanced up, looking like a kid being caught with his hand in the cookie jar. Normally, Max would have called the cocky kid out on it and yanked the red beauty out of his grasp, but nothing felt normal at the moment. The guitarist desperately needed an outlet, so he grabbed another acoustic from the closest rack and sat beside Will on the sectional. He matched the young man, chord for chord before taking over the jam session altogether.

Max let the moody riffs replace the more upbeat ones Will had been beckoning from the guitar, releasing all of his agitation through music. Will watched on cautiously from the corner of his eye, but chose wisely to offer no words. Even though the crowd liked to rag Will for being an eighteen-year-old idiot sometimes, he had the instinctual trait of being able to read other's emotions spot on. He witnessed Max's own dark set of emotions and held firmly to being an outlet and anchor for his friend without any commentary.

Will remained by Max's side on that couch until the torrent of misery subsided to a dull, more manageable storm of grief. Max slowly lifted his lethargic body from the couch and shuffled into his bedroom, praying slumber would show up and give him a break from the disarray of his life.

• ♫ • ♫ • ♫ •

A sharp pain struck between the middle of Max's shoulder blades, jolting him out of a restless sleep. His eyes shot open to find moonlight ghosting over the room. Before he could roll over, another jolt of pain was delivered, this time closer to his right kidney. His hip flinched away from the affliction.

"What the…" He looked over his shoulder, finding the outline of a little intruder wedged against him. He managed to ease onto his back before pushing his visitor over a bit. The kid was like lead. "What's wrong, little man?"

Ludwig rubbed his eyes, lips pouted out. "I want you to sing."

Chuckling gruffly, Max grabbed his phone from the nightstand and sent Mave a text. *Bug in my bed*.

Mave's reply was immediate. *Don't call him that! On my way*.

Max's groggy fingers fumbled over the keys. *No worries. He's good here*.

You sure?

Yep FYI, he will always be my bug.

Whatever.

Before Max could set the phone down, Ludwig was pulling on his arm. "Sing lullaby, Unca Max."

Max considered himself the weakest vocalist of the band, and it baffled him to no end why his nephew preferred him to always sing over the others. But if that was what the toddler needed, Max wouldn't question it that night.

He settled onto his pillow and opened his arm. "Okay, Bug. Come here."

The little guy happily snuggled into the crook of his uncle's arm. As Max began to croon the lyrics to Jack Johnson's "Lullaby," Ludwig's chubby fingers reached over and began rubbing Max's earlobe. It was something else the little guy only did with Max. Ludwig chose his uncle's ear as his security blanket well before he took his first step. Max liked to tease the crowd, saying it was because he had superhero ears. He knew better, but his nephew setting him apart from the rest truly did make him feel like a superhero.

The melody came out sleepy and a bit rough, but somehow did the trick. The toddler began snoring like a grown man before Max repeated the chorus. His voice trailed off and a tight knot wove around his chest as he ran his hand through Ludwig's fine brown hair. *How could my dad walk away from this?* He held the little boy tighter, not being able to fathom a life away from his niece and nephew. The love he held deeply for them was so visceral, and they were not even his own children.

Somewhere in the house, a clock struck on the midnight hour, reminding Max how precious time was and how his own father chose to squander his away from them. The resentment over his childhood threatened to overwhelm him. His voice trembled with the hurt as he began to pray.

"My heart hurts. I don't even think it belongs to me anymore." The words stuttered as tears burned the back of his throat. "God, you gotta help me. I need to be freed from this. I'm hurting…"

Ludwig's little leg shot out and nailed Max in the kneecap as his arm lashed out and popped him in the cheek. Both inflicted minor pain, but Max heard God loud and clear.

Yes, you're hurting, but it's not that bad.

A snort released from his nose at the same time as Ludwig let out a snarl from his tiny one. "Okay, I get ya." He cradled the squirmy toddler in his arms and thanked God for the precious gift of having the kid in his life. "Little Pearl, too. And all the other Bleu rugrats."

His prayer of thanks eventually trailed off when a long yawn released from his lips. Settling down, the night finally rested its head.

Morning tickled Max awake at dawn.

No, someone was tickling Max awake.

"Stop, Bug," he mumbled, eyes remaining closed. His hand flicked out to shoo the tickling away, but proved to be fruitless when the tickling along his arm started right back up. "Knock it off, little dude."

The growl of his voice did no good either. A giggle that was all female finally pulled his eyes open, finding a little brunette beauty with a thick blonde streak nestled amongst the waves of hair. It's as though Pearl couldn't decide between her mom's light hair color or her dad's dark, so she picked both. It gave her an ethereal appearance, or more closely, a wicked one at the moment in Max's opinion.

Clearing his throat, he watched on as she worked a bright-blue marker against his arm. "Whatcha doing, baby girl?"

She kept her focus on his arm and replied, "Coloring."

"Why would you color on me?" He pulled his arm away. "Stop."

She looked up at him, one of her tiny eyebrows lining the top of her big brown eyes arched in a grownup fashion. "But Unca Dillon said I could." Her little hand reached over and grabbed his arm, pulling it over his lap so she could finish the colorful scribbling.

A low chuckle sounded from the armchair by the door where Dillon sat sipping his coffee. He wore a simple pair of track pants and a splotchy pink tank top. Lifting the cup in greeting, he said, "Good morning, punk."

With his glower firmly trained on his wicked buddy, Max yanked his arm away once again. "Enough coloring on me, Pearl. Go find you some paper."

Giggling, she jumped off the bed and skipped toward the door, but Dillon's outstretched arm halted her. He turned his palm up and wiggled his fingers for the markers.

"But I want 'em," she whined.

"How's about I promise you that Aunt Jewels will go buy you a big set of washable markers after breakfast?"

The *washable* tidbit caught Max's attention. "The ones she's already got ain't washable?" His brows pinched together as Dillon's danced up and down in satisfied silliness.

The menacing growl ripping from Max's gritted teeth had the toddler dropping the fistful of contraband in Dillon's palm before she hurried out of the room. At the same time, Ludwig sat up in the bed and rubbed the sleep from his eyes to see what all the fuss was about.

"I wanna color, too," he said, eyeing Pearl's artwork along his uncle's arm.

Dillon snagged the neon-green one from the others and slowly spelled out, "P-E-R-M-A-N-E-N-T." He placed the markers in his pocket as he presented Max with a pointed look. "Nope. Not washable. Permanent like the pink on all my shirts."

Max looked down at the vivid scribbles competing with the sheet music. They looked as deeply rooted into his skin as the ink of the tattoo. "Seriously? Man, we got a concert

175

tonight."

Dillon's lips curved up wickedly, dimples showing up to taunt as well, as he brought the cup to his mouth. After he took a satisfying sip, he stood. "The trainer will be here shortly. Want me to take Bug back to his Pop so you can try getting that mess off of your arm?"

"Laugh it up now, punk. I'll get you back." Max scrubbed his hands along his bearded face. Before dropping his arm, the bright mess along his skin caught his eye, causing him to cringe.

Dillon easily swept Ludwig up and headed for the door. "Go ahead and you'll get burned again, Pepper Man."

It took until nearly the end of the summer to get Max back for the shirt prank, but Dillon had always been a patient man.

TEN

"Losing My Religion"
-R.E.M.

Five sets of determined eyes continued their showdown with one set of extremely unenthusiastic ones.

"No," Max repeated. His eyes had had enough, relenting to look away first so he could go back to studying the pizza he'd been shoveling in before he was so rudely interrupted.

The rest of the crowd had already finished their late lunch and was back to playing in the pool. Max glanced out the large set of windows and watched the bronzed group splish and splash with no worries in the world. The summer had warmed their skins several shades and lightened their hair in contrast, looking refreshed and carefree. He wanted to abandon his troubles in the newly decorated aqua kitchen and join them, but his struggles kept him tethered to the barstool.

"We're talking about one hot, leggy, blonde bombshell!" Trace nearly whined, his light-blue eyes wide to emphasize the point.

"Heard you the first time," Max grouched out around a mouthful of savory goodness. "No."

"It would help to get the hounds off of Mona's heels. I think it's the least you could do considering all she's done for you in the last year." Tate shot him a stern look. He pushed his phone across the island and pointed at the picture on display.

The cheesy, garlic ambrosia turned to sawdust on Max's tongue as he glanced at the screen, seeing again how happy Mona looked on the arm of some New York bigwig. Her eyes no longer held the anxiety he'd placed there. With her head slightly angled back, laughing, she looked healthier, too. The picture should have only given him comfort that she was able to move on, but it only rolled a thick wave of nausea through him, knowing another man was able to accomplish where he had failed.

Tossing the half-eaten slice of pizza back into the box, Max huffed in defeat. "Fine. Set it up. Make it happen."

Tate was the man for making it happen, and that's exactly what he done before that afternoon had time to settle into the day. A few phone calls had the date lined up and a few photographers the privilege of knowing ahead of time where the date was happening that very night.

"Please tell me that's not what you're wearing?" Tate questioned from the doorway of Max's room.

Max glanced down at the beat-up jeans with a few holes while trying to unsuccessfully rub the wrinkles from his blue V-neck. "What's wrong with this?"

"You look worn out, but we need to present you looking fresh and happy." Tate pushed his hand through his dark-red hair, clearly at his wits end with the indifferent guitarist.

"You know you just sounded like the biggest pansy," Max shot back as he watched his manager storm over to the closet and sort through the wardrobe filled with more of what he was already wearing.

Shaking his head, Tate gave up and rushed back out. Max relaxed against the headboard and began restringing a beat-up acoustic he lucked up finding when he and Will snuck out the night before to wander around some pawnshops along the boardwalk. By the time he had the new strings tightened, Tate was back with an armful of clothing. He tossed them, covering the guitar resting in Max's lap.

"Put them on and brush your hair and teeth." His demand left no room for argument. Tate eyed his friend's lower face. "Any chance of talking you into shaving."

Max shook his head to dismiss that request. "And I already brushed my teeth." He bared a set of perfectly white, straight teeth. He sorted through the clothes, finding a pair of black jeans, a crisp white T-shirt, and charcoal-grey vest. "How's Mave's clothes any better than what I'm already wearing?"

"They're wrinkle and hole free. Get them on. Sonny will be here in ten to pick you up." Tate headed for the door, but reiterated, "And don't forget the hair. Some gel goes a long way."

Hair freshly gelled into a manageable disarray and the borrowed outfit helped Max resurrect his chilled façade. Slouching in the back of the limo, he glanced out the tinted window as Sonny pulled up in front of a small condo. He remained in the limo, allowing his bodyguard to retrieve his blind date. The show wouldn't begin until they reached the restaurant anyway, so Max felt no need to begin any earlier.

A blonde emerged, looking overly spray-tanned. Her tangerine dress not helping the effect. One glance and Max was completely unimpressed.

"Guess this'll make one heck of a show," he muttered as the door opened, revealing unnatural green eyes and a set of glaring veneer teeth. *Fake.* The word described his date to a T.

"Hi, I'm Keekee." Her nasally voice grated him instantly. Without warning, she launched herself into his arms.

Max held his hands away from her, making it clear he would not be reciprocating the embrace as he gawked at Sonny. The bodyguard shrugged his thick shoulders before closing the door. Next thing he knew, the bubbly blonde whipped her phone out and snapped a selfie of them both.

"Umm… I'm Max—"

"I know who you are, silly!" Keekee reached over with a long acrylic nail and tapped the tip of his nose with the sharp point.

He gently pushed the overly affectionate woman off his lap and scooted over. There had been some pretty aggressive women over the years, so he knew how to handle them, but it held no appeal. While she reapplied a thick layer of gloss, he pulled his own phone out and sent a group message to the band and Tate that he would be bringing home a gun to deal with them later on. His phone chimed with several replies to his threat, but they went ignored.

Thankfully, the restaurant was close by so he only had to endure being trapped in the back with Miss Plastic for a short time. She carried on and on about her launching a fashion blog—how original—and how she was an extra in a music video for a band he had not recognized. When he admitted that, Max got another nose tap from her index claw.

"Out you go, darlin'," Max drawled out while helping Keekee from the back of the limo. Flashes took off, reminding him of strobe lights, as the paparazzi descended upon them.

Keekee needed no guidance, wrapping her ultrathin body against his side as they walked to the door. She even delivered a sticky kiss to his bearded cheek. As the door closed behind them, he tried to discreetly wipe the mess off, feeling it gumming up his beard.

"Ooh. This place is so high class," Keekee said on a squeal while snapping another selfie. Her fingers worked rapidly with captioning it to some social site.

"We can head somewhere a little more laidback—"

"No way!" She squeezed his arm, the tip of those daggers pinching his skin.

Everything was draped in white linen and crystal. It looked like he was going to pay dearly in the pocket for the exasperating date. Shoot, he'd triple the price tag to get out of the meal altogether if it were possible.

The host ushered them to a table in the middle of the dining area, placing them on full display. Max knew this was part of the show Tate set up, so he settled into the chair and got busy looking over the menu.

"Can we start you off with a beverage?" The waiter was there before the host finished placing Keekee in her chair.

"What'll ya have, darlin'?" Max motioned for her to order.

"White wine. Your best!" Her giddiness barely registered on her tight face, but it coated that nasally voice.

"And for you, sir?" The young guy eyed Max, looking like he wanted to join the rock star for supper, but he was professionally holding it together.

"You got tea?"

"Yes."

"Sweet?"

"No." His voice quivered a bit with having to disappoint the famous musician.

"Of course not, but that'll work."

The waiter hurried off, and Max began looking over the menu. He glanced up when his date released an irritated snort.

"You're not going to have a drink with me?"

"No, sweet thang, I am not. But you enjoy." As if his words summoned her glass, it appeared along with his glass of tea.

Max took a sip of the bland tea and set it back down dissatisfied. Before he could go back to searching the menu, another terse snort sounded.

"What is all over your arm?" Keekee's nose held a few wrinkles of disgust as she eyed his arm, but her forehead remained unnaturally smooth. Before he could answer, she was snagging another picture of him and sending it on its social media way.

Max ignored the growing irritation of all things Keekee, choosing to grin down at the fading scribbles, instead. "My niece drew on me." His shoulder shrugged a *so-what*, daring her to snort again. He reached for his glass and took another swig.

Keekee brushed her severely straight hair over her shoulder and leaned forward, those garishly green eyes gleaming. "I have edible paint. I'd love to paint you, and I'd let you paint me." Her talons drew a line down her exposed cleavage.

Max choked on his tea. He was baffled and repulsed at the same time that she took him talking about his niece coloring as a segue into propositioning him.

Clearing his throat several times, he finally shot it down. "No thanks."

Keekee exhaled another nasally huff.

"Do you need a tissue?" Max couldn't refrain from asking. He wondered if the obvious nose job was the culprit or had the chick always been inflicted with that awful sounding vocal lilt. She sounded like someone was pinching her nostrils shut.

"Why no. I do need an explanation on why this isn't appealing to you?" She motioned those long nails the length of her body in an offering. Without waiting for his response, she turned her phone on selfie mode and produced a ridiculous duck face—lips puckered and eyes psycho-wide.

He pulled his own phone out, snapping a picture of her posing for her camera. Disregarding several responses to the earlier message, he added the picture and—*Where did Tate find this narcissistic freak?* After pocketing the phone, he bowed his head and silently begged God to get him through the nightmare.

"Are you one of those *religious* people?" Revulsion fastened to the word religious as though it was a nasty term, and that was Max's undoing.

Looking up, he saw red. *Let the show begin...*

"Actually, I am." When she said nothing, he rattled off, "I'm Jehovamethaptist."

"Oh *gawd*. Are you serious?" Her nose managed another scrunch, but the rest of her face remained frozen.

Max threw politeness out the window and went for full-blown maniacal, knowing it would be much more fun. "Sure, sure. We have these great tent revivals. There's one this weekend. You should come with me. Lots of selfie opportunities."

"I'd rather not." Fear lit those fake green eyes.

He found the whole charade a bit too enjoyable and took it even further. His hands rose toward Miss Plastic as he allowed his eyes to close, giving the impression of reading her. "Oh no…"

"What?"

Panic in her voice had his eyes popping back open.

"The spirit is tellin' me you're possessed by a materialistic demon. That ain't good." Before the ditzy woman could process the underlying insult he just delivered, Max plowed on in the thickest southern drawl he could muster. "If we can get you to my priest and get ahold of a snake, we can fix you right up."

Her eyes grew as big as saucers as she stuttered, "No. That's okay."

"No worries. We can take care of it right here." Max dunked his fingers into his glass, and then flicked drops of tea on her as he shouted, "Flee demon!"

He had captured the attention of the entire restaurant by then and many camera phones were directed toward the show.

"Shouldn't you use holy water," she asked, trying to dodge the spray.

"Nah. Tea works just as good for vanity. It'd be even better if it was sweet," he grouched out as the wary waiter sidled up to the table. With Max's words, the guy ignored the russet splatters staining the pristine-white tablecloth and hurried back off.

Keekee was too wrapped up in trying to shield her hair from the tea shower to catch his jab. "That's enough! You're ruining my Brazilian blowout. It cost a fortune!"

Max dried his fingers, conceding to her demand. "I'm gonna light a candle for your soul."

"Isn't that the Catholic religion?" She glared at him, finally catching on to the ruse.

He held his palms up. "I ain't got nothin' against them folks. If any of 'em wanna light a candle for me, I ain't stoppin' 'em." The twang of his dialect became even more pronounced the more riled up he became.

And there went another nasally snort, along with an eye roll.

"You wanna tweet something, how about this?" He didn't even have to pause before she had the phone ready. "Nothing ticks me off worse than someone trying to label my faith in

God. It's not a religion. It's a relationship. You'd be wise to work on one with Him before looking for one with a man."

She looked up in confusion. "But that's too many characters for Twitter."

Max smacked himself in the forehead hard enough to leave a handprint. "I give up." After tossing three hundred-dollar bills onto the table, he stood and pulled his phone out to call Sonny. "Hey. I'm out. Please give Kinky—"

"It's Keekee!"

"—a ride home." Max walked away without so much as a goodbye, ignoring her whiny protests that followed him all the way out the front door.

The blinding flashes were instant. Max rubbed his eyes to rid them of the floaters as the paparazzi circled him like a pack of lions going in for the kill.

"Where's your hot date?" one shouted from the midst of chaos.

"Are you feeling ill, Max?"

"Something got you upset, man?"

Max produced a knowing smirk just to mess with them, not realizing it would come back to bite him in the butt. He walked down the sidewalk in a cocky swagger until almost tripping over one of the photographers blocking his way.

"Whoa, man." Max held his hand out, grabbing the guy on the shoulder to help him from landing on his aggravating backside. After he had the guy secured in an upright position, Max continued on.

"Thanks, Max," the guy called out like they were the best of pals.

Max kept strutting away and the pack kept persistently circling him. He pulled his phone out and shot Will a text. The kid had turned out to be his lifeline that summer with Mona's exit. A tinge of foreboding struck him, knowing his lifeline would be heading to college too soon. *How am I not going to sink?*

He shook that discomforting thought off and focused on getting out of the current sticky situation. He typed quickly. *Trapped in Beverly Hills. Rescue me with my truck.*

Will replied quickly. *Where?*

Max scanned for a road sign and text his location to his rescuer and then added—*Park in a nearby alley. Sit tight until I find you.*

The paparazzi were still shouting out questions and comments, mostly inappropriate. Dizzying chaos was escalating, pushing the musician to a precipice of panic. A song bubbled through Max's pursed lips from out of nowhere, giving the group an impromptu performance of his best Ray Charles impersonation.

"*Georgia…*" Max bellowed out the lyrics to "Georgia On My Mind" while the crowd halted in abrupt silence. He seemed to be full of spontaneous shows that night. Thankfully, this one seemed to put the frenzied mob into a trance.

His eyes swept over the swanky neighborhood. It sparkled in too much glam and pageantry, reminding him he was only a visitor. The charade of celebrity was not the real Maxim King and this egotistical part of California was not his home.

Homesick.

It struck so sharp against his heart as he screeched out the lyrics that his hand rushed to grasp his chest, begging the wound to hold together. The pain so violent, surely there would be no way to survive it.

"*Keeps Georgia on my mind…*"

Overwhelmed by the grief of missing home, the persistent threat of tears stung his eyes. Although it was well into the dark of night, Max grabbed the shades dangling from the front of his borrowed vest and swiftly pulled them on to mask his emotions. Rapid flashes of cameras firing off indicated he wasn't fast enough with his shield. Worry tickled his throat, but a harsh cough rid it, knowing it was futile to dwell on it.

"Max, man, are you okay?" the paparazzi feigned sincere concern over his state, hoping for an exclusive scoop. Others began spewing out their own inquiries with realizing the impromptu performance had concluded as hastily as it had begun.

With bleary eyes that were quite useless as a guide, Max entered the first door he pushed on. Oblivious to his surroundings, he stumbled through a dimly lit bar. Soft jazz music easily mingled with the languid chatter, along with a few gasps of recognition adding to the racket as he made his way to the back on a clear mission to escape.

"It's Maxim King!" a woman squealed.

"Let me buy you a drink, man!" a man shouted toward his retreating back.

"That concert last week was amazing!" a breathless woman said.

Keeping his chin tucked down and shades concealing his eyes, Max threw a hand up in recognition, but rushed to a side exit without glancing back.

The heat of the night vanished in an odd

vortex as the dark skies opened up to allow a sudden rain shower to meet him in the alleyway. Of course, this was not the one Will had found to hide down. Max was instantly soaked to the bone, feeling even more weighed down. His legs kept propelling him forward in a clipped pace, wanting to outrun the heavy clouds of dreadful defeat.

I'm going to drown…

ELEVEN

"Move (Keep Walkin')
-tobyMac

Five sets of weary eyes continued their showdown with one set of extremely unenthusiastic ones. The same five sets from yesterday, except Ben was now in Tate's place at the meeting. And the meeting table had moved from the kitchen to the back deck.

"No," Max repeated. The breeze danced through his hair, but the clouds continued to stingily hide the sun. He severed his stare first, thinking he needed to focus on finding his own sunshine.

"You need to clean up the dumb mess you

made last night." Ben's tight tone gave no wiggle room for Max to find an out.

Max looked back at his other manager, thin lips pressed in a severe line, deep lines marring his forehead. He wondered if Tate put his foot down and demanded Papa Bear Ben to handle the latest fiasco.

"Maxim," Mave said in a quiet warning.

"Look, all I did was goof off a little bit last night. The world is going to think whatever they want. A statement from me ain't gonna change it." His eyes swept over the grey waves crashing onto the shore.

"I didn't know you were Jehovamethaptist." Trace scratched the side of his blond head.

"I'm not, Space Cadet. I made it up." Max couldn't stifle the eye roll before it escaped.

The group snickered, but Ben cleared his throat in warning before addressing Max once again. "You need to apologize for making fun of religion. That's a vast community you slammed last night with the restaurant exorcism."

Snorts joined the conversation from his bandmates, but cut off abruptly when Ben delivered a scolding look.

"Fine," Max muttered, conceding to pay

the repercussions for his stunt.

Blake pulled up the notepad app on his iPad to dictate Max's statement. The young assistant had matured over the last few years, proving all the members of the band wrong, and completely proving Jewels right as always.

Max began once Blake gave his head a nod. "I made up Jehovamethaptist as a joke that I am now realizing was in poor taste. God is far greater than any title we like to slap on our relationship with Him." He paused to let Blake catch up typing. Once Blake looked up, Max began again. "The only religious organization I belong to is the Dirt Roads Faith of Tiny Town Church where silicon fruit-loops are sacrificed as burnt-out offerings."

Ben groaned loudly, but was drowned out by the raucous laughter overtaking the rest of the group.

Shoving his fingers through his grey hair, Ben leveled Max with a look of exasperation. "Well, you took it serious for all of two seconds. And that's two seconds longer than I expected." He moved his attention to Blake, whose hands hovered over the screen with needing direction. "Only keep the first two sentences and add, 'I apologize if I offended anyone.'"

"Funny, man. You are a member of a *Baptist* church back home." Logan pointed out.

"That's not the *point*." Max scowled at no one in particular.

"We get it. The chick made fun of your faith and it struck a nerve." Dillon waved his hand to dismiss it. "Let's move on."

"Max, if you need a break, we are fine with it. Will can finish out the last few concerts for you." Ben's harsh features softened.

Apparently, the topic had already been discussed without Max. He glanced around the table and was met with understanding, steady gazes. He shook his head. "Nah, man. All's good as long as you idiots don't set me up on anymore blind dates."

Trace huffed. "We were just trying to have your back. You and Mona just broke up and the chick is already out there flaunting a new guy—"

"No, we didn't! I ended things last year. It's all on me. Leave her alone!" His rage bellowed out of him, effectively silencing the group. Ashamed over his outburst, Max sucked in several deep breaths of the salty air to calm himself. The guys had his best interest at heart, he knew, and they didn't deserve him taking his stress out on them.

"The media doesn't see it that way," Ben added.

"Well, the media can kiss my—"

"Enough!" Dillon interceded. "Get it together or head on back to Georgia."

"It's three gigs. I'll finish. What else can go wrong in that little bit of time?" Max allowed his shoulder to shrug up in an arrogant twitch, full of attitude. He shoved away from the table and continued doing what he'd been doing all summer—running away from his problems. But this time, his pursuit of escape had him colliding with Kyle in the foyer.

"They done with your scolding already?" Kyle's green eyes danced in tease as he placed a suitcase beside several other more feminine ones by the door.

"I set those punks straight."

Kyle smirked. "Yeah, right."

Sunshine time. Max looked between his friend and the large black suitcase thoughtfully before heading to his truck. Kyle and the girls were set to fly back to New York the next day, so Max focused on a parting gift for the newlyweds instead of his overwhelming life.

"You should have known better than to say something as stupid as, 'What else can go wrong?'" Mave growled, throwing the magazine on the driftwood coffee table.

"When are you going to learn that your dumb pranks always backfire?" Dillon muttered while thumbing through another magazine. "Massage oil, lingerie, fury handcuffs... Man, some of this stuff makes me blush too much to say out loud. Were you trying to embarrass Kyle or get him kicked off the flight?" He looked up with an arched brow, his indigo eyes hard.

Max shrugged, realizing he didn't quite think this one all the way through. He had replaced all of Kyle's suitcase belongings with a treasure trove of naughty items, thinking about how hilarious it would be to see the look on Kyle's face when he went through the luggage check at the airport.

Kyle had text him—*Thanks for making me look like a pervert. I'll get you back for this!*

The thought didn't even cross Max's mind that someone would find out about his little shopping spree. The clerk at the adult store happily shared a copy of Max's receipt with several gossip rags. The guy also shared a few fuzzy pictures he snagged with his phone showing the guitarist hiding his face ineffectively under a cowboy hat while strolling down an aisle of inappropriate paraphernalia, causing a full force media explosion, so severe they were still feeling the aftershocks a few days later.

Maxim King from the legendary band Bleu Streak has had one wild week in Southern California. He went on record to profess his faith in God one day after making a mockery of the religious community, and was caught shopping for a gross amount of sleazy lingerie and sex toys the next. Photos have also surfaced of a glassy eyed King entering a bar after causing a scene in a nearby restaurant in Beverly Hills. Is he following in his father and brother's footsteps? Will Maxim King be heading to rehab next?

"This is very damaging." Tate shook his head while reading over the story.

Max shrugged again and muttered around chewing on his thumbnail. "I just wanted to have some fun at Kyle's expense."

"Well, your shenanigans have been considerably costly." Ben looked at another headline Blake had just pulled up on his laptop and sighed heavily. It declared Max a drunk like his father. "What were you even doing in a bar in the first place?"

"The paparazzi were hounding me, man! I was trying to get away from them, so I ran in the front door and out the back to hide," Max snapped.

Ben turned the laptop screen around to show Max the image of himself looking beyond wasted—eyes red and squinting with his cheeks flushed. It was taken at the moment he had been about to drop his basket and cry in front of everyone. If he didn't know better, Max would believe the story the photo portrayed as well.

"And this is just as lovely," Tate said, hitting the YouTube video of Max singing a garbled rendition of "Georgia On My Mind."

"Dude," Trace mumbled with worry, his face turning pale.

Max cringed with embarrassment, but anger pushed the shame aside and took over. His jaw flexed as the words charged out of his mouth. "If I was drinking, that's *my* business, but I wasn't. Truth of the matter, I was about to cry like a baby 'cause I'm *homesick*." He sniffed the recurring threat back and blinked several times to get himself in check. "I don't think I have to explain the hatred I have toward alcohol, since all you punks know what I've lived through with my father *and* brother."

Silence blanketed the group as they watched him push out of the chair and stalked over to his room, slamming the door hard enough to rattle the hinges. The bang was so loud, it even made the commotion upstairs hesitate for a few seconds. Soon the children went back to their squeals and laughter while sounding like a stampede. Their jovial demeanor couldn't have been more opposite of the somber crowd sitting around on the first floor. Each guy sat glaring at the floor while concentrating on how they could help Max out. One by one, they eventually meandered upstairs to get away from the tension.

The day crept by until night took over. Max was a no-show for a radio interview and a scheduled practice with the band, but no one dared to bother him. Mad as he was, his stomach wouldn't let him stay hidden. As he shuffled out the door to find something to eat, he glanced at the broken iPad and iPhone where both laid crumbled along the bottom of the bedroom wall. Each headline of him being a nympho alcoholic riled him into a bitter rage until both electronic devices became victims of it.

The fact that he had never been drunk irritated the entire situation even further. On his way to the kitchen, he mimicked what he'd witnessed on TV and a few times in person from Martin as well as Mave. Zigzagging and staggering into furniture along the way. His arm even managed to sloppily turn over a lamp. It clanged to the floor in protest, but he didn't even pause to pick it up since the thing somehow managed to remain in one piece. As he fake-groveled around to grasp the fridge handle, he heard steps come up behind him.

"Tell me you ain't drunk!" Dillon demanded, his deep voice rumbled out.

Max turned to offer his best intoxicated impression, head bobbing around while wearing a toothy grin so wide it squinted his eyes to slits.

His giant friend dropped to the floor, wrapped his arms around his long drawn-up legs and began rocking dramatically. "Not happening. This is not happening," he began to chant in time with his rocking.

Max snorted and motioned for him to get up. "You're too big of a man to pull off that pansy act."

Dillon stood, towering over him. "Yeah. And you're too smart of a man to be pretending to be a drunken idiot."

"Well, I'm being accused of everything

under the sun. Figured since we're in Hollywood I'd go ahead and play the role. Staggering drunk or invalid on my deathbed. Pick one." Another picture of him leaving a follow-up appointment with his doctor had headlined that he was hiding another, more serious illness and only had a few months to live.

"I pick that you use the good sense God gave ya."

"I'm just so sick of it, man!" Max threw his hands in the air, exasperated. A single tear rebelled against his demand to stay put and escaped down his bronzed cheek. As he swiped the tear away, he heard his mom's voice trying to calm him as a young child. It was after she had finally dried her own tears and was trying to convince him to do the same. *Your soul is much too beautiful to continue to cry.* In the present moment, all he felt was ugly. Ugly heart, ugly choices, ugly consequences...

"This is our reality, especially while we're out here in California." Dillon pointed to the barstool and took one himself at the kitchen island.

A large coral sculpture rested in the middle of the new granite countertop Leona called Waterland Terra Aqua. It actually looked exactly like the ocean in motion. Both men's eyes followed the undulating pattern in silence for a few beats.

Dillon continued after a while. "One, we're celebrities whether we want to admit it or not. Two, our checking accounts tend to spawn enough jealously on their own. Three, we confess to be Christians. Max, that target on our back is so vast, a blind man with no aim could hit it." He extended his arms wide, filling the space with his wingspan, to make his point.

Max eyed him, making no comment.

Dillon's eyes gleamed with emotion as he spoke, "Let them say stupid stuff. Let their jealousy push them into taunting us. Let their simplemindedness dismiss our faith." He clamped his large hand tight to Max's shoulder. "But don't let them rob you of your joy and peace. Jesus went through way too much for us to be squandering our freedom. This is a storm in your life. And like all storms, it'll pass."

Max shook his head. "I know... I just... This storm didn't just plow through. It set up shop to stay." Another tear silently trekked down his face, but he nudged it away with wanting to conceal it from Dillon. "I'm tired of the clouds. When am I ever going to feel the sun again?"

"'You are the light of the world. A town built on a hill cannot be hidden,'" Dillon whispered one of his favorite verses to his friend, Matthew 5:14. "You've got that sun inside you. It's up to you to let it out."

"I've forgotten how."

"I don't know why you let your old man screw with your head so bad when he showed back up last year."

"He didn't mess with my head. He ruined my heart." Max pressed his hand against the pain swelling in his chest. He sucked in several shaky breaths before he could continue. "I think it's time to go home... I need to go home..." A sob stuttered from his damp lips, but he managed to hold the tears back.

"I understand. I'll have Blake get you on the first flight out. Go pack." Dillon nodded his head toward the stairs.

Max didn't make a move. "I'm quitting y'all."

"You're not quitting. You know it's time for you to move on from this and staying in California ain't cutting it. You're wellbeing is far more important than a few gigs. It's only a week and we'll be back home, too." Dillon pulled his phone out and hit Blake's contact. "Yo. Book Max a ticket home on the next available flight," he spoke into the phone and paused to listen. "Thanks, man."

Max pushed away from the island and walked to the stairs. Dillon was right. It was time to sort things out. Dillon called out before he descended the stairs.

"'For just as we share abundantly in the suffering of Christ, so also our comfort abounds through Christ.' Don't forget to lean on Him. You're not alone in this, Max."

Max tossed his hand up in acknowledgement, knowing his voice wouldn't be able to penetrate past the pain flooding him.

It was definitely time to go home.

TWELVE

"Broken"
-Lifehouse

"Tiny Town"
-Finding Favour

The red eye from LAX to Atlanta was swathed in an eerie calm after such an uproar in the airport earlier when Max was checking in just before midnight. The place had become a frenzy of fans wanting to know how Max was doing. Also, an elderly lady took it upon herself to scold him for his inappropriate prank, telling him he was raised better than that. It was a blessing and burden to be Maxim

King. He had always opened himself to the fans, wanting to be personal with them. This made them all view him as a member of their own family. But their curiosity and concern was too much for him to handle, so Max upgraded his usual coach ticket to first class so he could hide.

Hiding became overbearing as the quiet cabin whispered all of the chaos of his life in a spinning cycle of confusing questions.

How?

Why?

How did this mess happen?

Why did I allow it?

How can I clean it up?

Why can't I figure it out?

A fine sheen of sweat beaded on his forehead, beckoned forth by the pounding of each regret to his gut. His breath caught from the stabbing in his chest each time he tried to inhale. Swiping the perspiration from his upper lip, his fingers discovered the tremble of grief.

I'm falling apart…

Drowning…

Sinking…

A choked sob fell from his mouth without warning. His head jerked up, scanning around the dimly lit cabin to see if anyone caught it before it clattered to the floor. Most of the leather seats were reclined at the late hour. Thankfully, Max found no eyes witnessing his meltdown, so he kicked the offensive display of emotion under his seat and focused on keeping the sobs mute as tears fell in a mournful procession.

The realization hit him that he had not properly mourned the loss of innocence inflicted from the abandonment of his father. The fissure he'd been carelessly bandaging with whatever worked at the time finally rebelled and split wide open.

Unable to swallow it back down, Max's knees hit the floor of the plane before he could register his actions.

"Oh... God... Please... Please take this from me... I can't carry it anymore... It's ruining me. Ruining my life. Please... I need to forgive him... Help me forgive him... Heal me... Please heal me..."

His whispered prayers kept on a repetitious procession until they switched to Max begging God to heal Martin, to forgive Martin, to take Martin's burden of addiction away.

"Please... Please forgive and heal my dad of his

sins..."

The hollow ache drained away, leaving a numbing sensation after a while. Exhausted and cried out, Max climbed back into his seat as sleep pulled him under. Dreams flickered like old home videos, conjuring images of a happier time when growing up in a tiny town with dirt roads was more than enough.

• ♫ • ♫ • ♫ •

"Eight is a good age as any."

"Really?" Max asked hesitantly, unsure of his dad's suggestion. He kicked a rock into the ditch as they walked down the dirt road that ran behind their small trailer. The humid summer had their chestnut locks curling tight and cheeks a bit flushed.

"Sure. Nothing wrong with a little mischief for a good laugh. Go ahead."

"You ain't gonna let Momma take a switch to me, are ya?" Max chewed on his thumbnail and looked up at the tree his dad pointed at.

"No," Martin said on a deep laugh. "It'll teach your brother a good lesson."

Maverick thought it was okay to take Max's fishing pole without permission, and thought it was even more okay that he broke it.

It was an accident! He and Max had went around and around with the argument the day before, but nothing was resolved.

Max had whined to his dad about it until Martin suggested the little lesson.

"You gonna do it or not?" Mischief twinkled in Martin's hazel eyes.

The twins' grandpa had given both boys a new fishing pole and a tackle box filled with lures and hooks for passing the second grade their *second* time through. The sun caught on the line filled with all of the goodies from Mave's tackle box that Max had attached, making it cast sparkles against the dark dirt. It looked like a redneck Christmas garland.

Taking a deep breath, Max held tight to one end of the fishing garland as he scurried up the tree. It took him no time to have all of Mave's fishing supplies strung from the branches. He hopped down and followed his dad on to the corner store where they shared a bottle of icy cold cola and a good laugh over Max's first ever prank. A prank instigated by his very own father.

THIRTEEN

"If We're Honest"
-Francesca Battistelli

"Someday Never Comes"
-Creedence Clearwater Revival

Cleaner air, the humidity of summer, dust in the breeze, the languid rush of lake water...

Home. He was finally home.

The summer had felt closer to a decade long than just mere months. The weight of the last year was left somewhere over the middle of the U.S., so Max nearly floated into his lake house that was made up of three older cabins gathered together. Hudson, the trailer park manager, wanted to tear them down and build more energy sufficient ones, but Max talked him into moving them deeper in the wooded shore. The guitarist had a contractor transform them into his own little lakeside retreat. The first cabin was expanded and made up the main living quarters. The second one became a guest house and the third a guitar sanctuary.

Max shuffled into the main cabin and straight to bed to catch up on some sleep. It wasn't until he had slept the entire day away and spent a long time in the shower to wash it away that he noticed a few things around the house.

He wrapped a towel around his lean waist and went on a search for some sustenance to hush his growling stomach in the kitchen. Running his hand through his damp hair, Max bent to sniff the unexpected tray of peanut butter cookies on the counter. A note sat beside it to let him know Izzy had her mom send them over from her bakery. He picked one up and gave it a tentative lick. When it didn't set fire to his tongue, Max deemed the treat safe for consumption and inhaled a half dozen without pause. After finding a quart of milk waiting in the fridge and guzzling it, his eyes caught something else peculiar out of the back window that overlooked the other two cabins.

A light shined from the guest house.

Groaning, Max pulled on a pair of sweatpants and grabbed a bat to go welcome his unwelcomed guest. It wouldn't be the first time he'd found someone there. Normally it was some kid from the trailer park needing a break from their parents.

He hurried down the short stone path and cautiously eased the unlocked door open. "Hey. No worries if you ain't robbing me. Just come on out," Max said in an even tone, not wanting to spook the perpetrator.

The figure who padded around the corner caused him to drop the bat and gasp.

"You're the last person I'd expect to find here."

"Dillon called me… You've grown a beard?" Mona asked, standing barefooted in a pair of yoga pants and an oversized tee that fell off her shoulder. Her mahogany mane was piled high in a messy bun, and no makeup marred her features.

Max thought she looked so perfect it made him hurt.

He brushed the tips of his fingers along his scruffy cheek. "Going for the hipster look."

"You wear it well." Mona cleared her throat, looking nervous all of a sudden.

"Max—"

"I've missed you." He took a few steps closer, burning to hold her again.

"Then why'd you let me go?" Her voice was barely a whisper as her aqua eyes swam in tears.

"I was scared." His hands reached out and drew her against his chest.

"Of what?" She didn't protest, wrapping her arms around his waist.

"That you'd leave me first." A throaty chuckle escaped him with no evident humor. "Pretty lame, I know."

"All you had to do was talk to me about it. I get it, Max. What you went through with your father…"

Placing his fingers under her delicate chin, Max drew her attention up to meet his eyes. "Is it too late to talk about it now?" his hoarse voice pleaded.

"I'm here."

"What about your new guy?"

Her cheeks warmed to a lovely pink as she smiled wryly. "Just a client. I may have played that up a bit for the cameras."

"Always looking out for me, huh?" Max shook his head and placed an affection kiss to her forehead. He meant for it to be brief, but once his lips connected to her skin, he couldn't pull away.

They stood in each other's arms with his lips pressed to her forehead in a spell of regret and relief. Without thought, Max began leading them in a slow dance around the small cabin, just appreciating the moment he never imagined he'd have again. His lungs finally loosened and allowed deep breaths scented with her ever-present coconut to soothe him.

"Why didn't you just go to Vegas when I begged," he mumbled.

Mona lifted her head from his shoulder. "Because I didn't want you rushing into something you'd regret. I wanted to give you time to be sure."

"Baby, the only thing I regret is screwing things up with you."

"I'm here aren't I?"

"I don't deserve—"

"None of us deserves anything, but we all should appreciate and accept the gifts God has offered us." She traced his shoulder with her index finger before dropping her head back there.

"Let's go to Vegas now," he nearly begged.

Her giggle tickled along his bare skin. "No. You've had enough publicity lately."

"Seriously, Mona, I need to marry you." His gruff voice had her lifting her head once again.

"Hopefully, some day."

He realized she wasn't going to give him the answer he wanted nor deserved, so Max dropped it and indulged in just being with her again. He dipped his head toward her and stopped only a breath away from her parted lips to wait for permission. He wasn't stupid. Sure, he didn't grab up his gift like his brother, but he understood how precious Mona truly was to him.

When her lips finally lined with his, Max groaned in pure relief and pulled her closer. Unrushed and gentle. Affectionate and devastatingly sweet. He kissed her until his lips felt raw, demanding the physical demonstration to give Mona what his words were incapable of, his profound apology for abandoning her and the promise to never do it again.

When she tried to extract herself from his arms he refused, worrying the fragile moment would shatter, leaving him abandoned again. *No!* He also refused his thoughts to go there.

"Mine," he whispered along her lips before kissing a path to the delicate skin of her neck.

Mona giggled again and pushed against his chest. "I think we need to calm down."

Foreheads resting against each other, both quietly caught their breath while keeping a close eye on the other. Max kept tamping down the relentless fear of her disappearing.

"I'm still hot. Come on," Mona declared as she pulled them in the direction of the back door.

He groaned again, but allowed her to lead him outside. Hand in hand, they ran down to the dock and jumped right off the end into the cool water. It had the effect needed, dousing the overwhelming need he had for her. Allowing the water to rinse away the dirt of the past few months, Max indulged in what a summer night on Shimmer Lakes could only provide. It gave him a safe haven to just be for a spell with no expectations, no facades to keep erect, and no fear of what's to come.

Time drifted on the soft flow of the water, until they eventually tired of swimming. A few hours followed with a long conversation about all of the events of the bizarre and tiresome summer while their clothes dried from the night's comforting warm breeze. As the sun began to peek around the edge of day, Max and Mona stretched out on the dock while Max strummed a guitar.

Home.

With his woman back in his arms and a guitar resting in her lap, Max felt it all the way to his bones. He was home.

Nothing could ruin the moment. Or that's what he thought until a car door slammed, *ruining* the perfect moment.

Max stopped strumming the guitar and looked back toward the cabin, unable to see who had arrived. "Who done and found me already?" he grouched out as they both stood to go find out. He grabbed Mona's hand and began trekking up the path.

"Dillon may have called someone besides me."

Max glanced over and found Mona looking rather sheepish. "What? Who?"

"Max, you need to give your father a chance," she whispered as Martin shuffled around the side of the cabin.

Then it dawned on him, sending a punch to his gut. Mona was just helping him out once again. "No wonder you won't say yes," he muttered, knowing she wouldn't be able to hear him from her current angle.

"What was that?" she asked, but he just shook his head.

"Good morning," Martin said, his voice weak and unsure.

In only wrinkled damp sweatpants, Max felt too vulnerable to have the needed conversation with his estranged father. "Come on in. I just need to change." He dropped Mona's hand and hurried inside without looking back.

Once he shrugged on one of his favorite V-neck tees and pair of jeans, he wandered out to the living room and only found Martin sitting in an oversized armchair. His father looked frail compared to the massive chair. Max's breath hitched when he realized it wasn't the chair's fault at all. Within mere weeks, Martin had lost more weight and his skin more jaundice than before.

Max hesitantly sat across from him and watched on as Martin stopped chewing his thumbnail, a habit they both shared he realized.

"I've been going to church with your momma," Martin confessed. "The preacher has been talking a lot about forgiveness lately... I don't deserve your forgiveness, but I sure would love to have it anyway. I'm sorry."

"For?"

"Everything."

Max shook his head and snorted. "Aren't we all?" They sat in silence until Max worked up enough nerve to ask the question that had haunted him most of his life. "Why weren't we worth staying for?"

A hiccup of remorse fell from Martin's thin lips. "Awe, son… I was no good for y'all."

Anger zipped through Max in a white-hot flash. "Don't give me that crap. Mave could have used the same lame excuse. Instead, he manned up to his addiction and got better."

"He had a support system—"

Max threw his palms up. "Again, a lame excuse. You had Momma and us boys."

"It wasn't fair to expect Judith to put up with me while trying to raise you two. Y'all were all I had and it was unfair to you. I did what I thought was best." It sounded as though it exhausted him to confess as much, his voice tapering off as his breathing became more labored.

"To abandon us… You thought *abandoning* us was for the best?"

"I'm not saying it was the right decision. It was the worst one of my life. I left thinking I'd get straightened out and come home. Only, things got worse…" He cleared his throat. "But I'm here now to say I'm sorry. I need your forgiveness. And I need you to get over it before it screws your life up, too."

"*Before* it does?" Max laughed bitterly, the rancid taste of his reality was appalling. "It already has!"

"Only if you allow it."

The conversation he had with Dillon mingled with the long prayer he shared with God on the plane, knowing Martin was right. Another long stretch of silence said more than they had managed to say with words. Both were hurt and both dwelling on the consequences. Beating themselves up until their lives were ragged from the abuse.

Max regarded the man before him until the anger transgressed to pity. Martin had lost, not him. He got what Martin couldn't grasp with the unconditional love of his mother and brother. And that love only came from God. Martin may have allowed his demons to run him off, but God had delivered a bevy of family in many shades and backgrounds. His Bleu family was a gift not many ever witness in this selfish world, but Max had. For that he was thankful as well as ashamed that he'd not shown Martin that love God placed in his heart many years ago.

Dillon was right. The light was in him all

along, but it was Max who stubbornly refused it to shine. It was time to let the clouds of the past to go. It was time to show Martin what true sunshine felt like.

"This," Max began, motioning between them, "ain't gonna fix in one conversation. I wish it were that easy."

Martin's eyes quivered with unshed tears as he slowly rose from the chair.

"But how about you come back tomorrow and we can work on it some more while we're fishing."

Martin looked back, surprised. "Yeah?"

Max nodded, acknowledging the fact that seeing his dad happy had pleased him so much. *Sunshine feels good. Let it out and warm your father.* "Yeah."

"I'll… I'll be here. Just say the time," Martin stuttered out, barely holding back his excitement.

It was so close to a childlike reaction that it struck Max deeply. Maybe his dad had missed out on more than anyone would ever realize due to his addiction demons. His frail body was testament to the fact he had paid dearly for it.

"It ain't true fishing if it doesn't happen before dawn," Max repeated the exact declaration Martin had shared with him and Mave long ago.

A weak laugh that turned into a sob sounded from Martin as he sluggishly lunged in to hug Max without permission. "I have no right to be back in your life. Thank you, son. I'm so proud that you've grown into the man I could never be. You're a good man." He released his stunned son and limped out the front door.

Gathering all of his scattered emotions, Max stood frozen for the longest time. His thoughts competed in a tug-of-war between Mona and Martin. In the end, the understanding that he had to fix what was broken with his father won out, so he amended with himself to leave her alone until he could be the man she deserved.

Max slipped on some shoes and went to a big fishing supply store to do what his dad couldn't when they were growing up, replacing something that broke with something better.

Max had to have a delivery truck drop off all the goods he planned on using to add sunshine to both his and his father's life. The material things weren't the sunshine, but they'd aid in the memories made. Time was but a vapor, and Max had already wasted enough of it living in a cloud of past sorrow. He had the overwhelming desire to push the clouds away so he and his dad could capture as many rays of life together as possible.

• ♪ • ♪ • ♪ •

With teeth bared and eyes set in a menacing glare, Mave released a nasty growl.

"No one brought this on you, but you. Fishing boats are for fishing. Not a jungle gym. Now suck it up." Dr. Carter inspected the gash marring the back of Mave's head as he meticulously added another staple.

Max and Martin watched on, looking like guilty parties with their sunburnt faces peeking from underneath their lopsided fishing hats.

Mave released another snarling growl. "I just wanted to get a better look at the sharks."

Max snorted. "They were *dolphins*."

"They looked like sharks to me. In my story they will be *sharks*." Mave's glower had Max hitching his shoulder. "These staples are worth it for sharks, not dolphins."

"Ain't we lucky Logan's uncle is a head doctor?" Max grinned, deepening his brother's frown.

With Will on fall break, a special trip had been planned. The entire band was in Charleston to accompany Martin to the tattoo parlor, so he could receive his family emblem on his hip. The long weekend was to be rounded out with a deep-sea fishing trip, but of course, Mave added an emergency room visit to the itinerary. The band was all camped out in a private waiting room somewhere in the hospital at the moment.

"I'm not sure I would use the word lucky in the same sentence with this gentleman." Dr. Carter looked up from Mave's head before going back to work. "I've heard many a tale."

Snap!

"GRRR!" Mave was sweating profusely, close to reaching his limit with the staple gun and the teases.

"Can't you give my son something? He's hurting." Martin was beyond upset.

Max patted his dad's shoulder. "He's a tough punk. He can take pain like a boss."

Mave responded with another guttural moan, causing Martin to wince.

The twin's dad had not been back in their lives very long, but he made it somehow feel like he'd always been there. Martin was genuine, wearing every infliction of his heart right there on his sleeve. He cried a lot, tears ranging anywhere from regret to joy. If the family was happy, Martin was happy. If his family was hurting, Martin hurt ten times worse for them. At the moment, he was close to shedding tears of anguish over his son suffering.

"Why not let the doc numb it at least?" Martin began worrying the nail on his trembling thumb.

"This is my consequence, Pop. I'd rather endure the pain than to even think about a relapse."

The tension sat heavy as the doctor popped in another staple.

"We need to start dressing you in bubble wrap," Martin declared in all seriousness, squirming in his chair.

"Ha! Dillon gave him a case of that stuff for Christmas one year." Max laughed.

Martin and Mave did not.

EPILOGUE

"My Story"
-Big Daddy Weave

As Preacher Mike Floyd stands at the podium in our small church, I come close to laughing but hold it in check. He adjusts the silly sun visor on his bald head, clearly uncomfortable about the bet he lost with Dad.

Mave leans around Momma, catching my attention and whispers, "Wonder where Pop even found that getup? I had no idea polo shirts came in polka dots." He wrinkles his nose while angling his head to check out more of the outfit.

"Shh!" Momma scolds as she pushes him to lean back so we can't continue our conversation.

I look back to our preacher and blink a few times to adjust to the brightness of his outfit. "He looks like he's wearing plaid bloomers," I mumble.

"They're called golf knickers," Trace, of all people, interjects from behind me where he sits on the second pew with the rest of the band. Mave and I both whip our heads around to eye him.

"What? It's true," Trace whispers.

"Them things are a neon rainbow of craziness. It hurts my eyes. I call them criminal." Momma nudges me too forcefully with her sharp elbow to hush me. "Oww!"

"How about I go ahead and address my attire so that maybe Mr. King can quieten down," Preacher Floyd says, rendering me mute. I jerk back around in the pew.

"That's Maxim, sir," Mave points out with an irritating smirk, sounding more like a punk kid than a grown man.

Our preacher squints over the top of his bifocals and studies the colorful tattoos covering Mave's arms. "I've gotten pretty good at telling the two of you apart." He redirected his attention to the rest of us. "On our last fishing trip, Martin made me promise he got to pick out my attire today if he out-fished me. Obviously, he did."

We join him in a round of laughs. Sounds like my old man. He became one lively somebody close to the end of his life. He donned a stubborn streak like the rest of us, declaring he would outlive the doctors' predictions so that he wouldn't miss meeting his next grandchild. He did and then some, spending the last month with us at my cabin so he could get to know Jameson.

Sniffing back the emotions, I lean over and kiss my infant son's soft head where it's resting in the crook of my wife's arm. She's right there so there's no denying a kiss to her damp cheek. Mona's eyes are rimmed red, missing my dad already, too. She offers me a smile before focusing back to our preacher.

"Today I'm here to tell you the story of Martin King. He was worried I'd get up here and sugarcoat his life. His words, not mine. Went as far as writing it down the way he wanted it told." Preacher Floyd holds up several sheets of paper and eyes each of us who are crowded on the front pew. Izzy and the twins beside Mave, Momma in the midst of us, Me, Mona and Jameson.

The preacher clears his throat and begins

reading.

"*Pretty sorry of me to completely destroy my life before knowing how to properly appreciate it. I lost out on a lot and it's all my fault. God gave me the world and all I did was make a mess of it. I wish this was being read to say that I was an upright man, devoted husband and father, but I was none of those things. I was a selfish alcoholic that chose my addition over supporting my family and it cost me everything. I can tell you that by some generous miracle from God, I got a second chance with my family. I didn't deserve it, but they gave it to me.*

Even though I ran away from my family, abandoning them to fend for themselves, my wife Judith prayed for me. Thirty years of praying and God heard her. Again, I didn't deserve her love and devotion, but she gave it. Judith, I love you, and thank you for praying for me.

Proud isn't a strong enough word to describe how I feel about my two sons. The talent them two have is pure magic. I'd like to say they got that from me, but I assure you I get no credit for their story. That came from them overcoming incredible odds and pure determination. They're both Godly men who don't claim to be perfect. They claim to be real and flawed like the rest of us and are humbled by their blessings. I look up to them and not because I'm shorter. No, those two have taught me a lot about life these last few years. Maxim and Maverick, I love you and want to thank you for forgiving me.

I'm a sinner. A sinner who ruined his gift of life. A sinner who got a second chance. We all sin and fall short, but I want to share with you how God forgave me anyway. And all I had to do was ask. None of us deserve it, but He loves us so much. In the small church where you sit today, God got ahold of me and I finally listened. My biggest regret was waiting so long to ask. Don't you let the demons of your life stop you from the gift it was meant to be. Ask God in. I did and was given peace in my last years of life. I got to love my family the way God intended for me to love them. My story is a mess, but God never gave up on me. My redemption is His story."

I wipe away my tears, thankful that God gave us all a second chance so many times. I have memories with my old man to hold on to. As Dillon plays one of my dad's favorite songs softly on the piano, I drift back several months to the concert we put on at the Shimmer Lakes Spring Festival. Pop snuck in the audience with Momma, thinking we wouldn't see them, but for some reason I've always been able to sense when he's around.

As soon as I caught sight of him, I set off in

a new riff and threw the entire concert out of order. Ben tossed his clipboard in the trash and let us have our way with the rest of the show. We jammed out to a list of all of my dad's favorites, dedicating the show in his honor. Our old man beamed with pride that night.

Dillon handed over the mic to Mave near the end of the show, and we brought the place down with a cover of Creedence Clearwater's "Down on The Corner" which was always one of our old man's favorites. Then we all crooned out a cappella "Stand By Me" after our bodyguards helped our parents to the stage, so they could share a dance to *their* song. It would end up being their last dance together.

Several shouts of praise draw me back to the piano where Dillon is laying claim to the keys while singing. My dad would have loved this.

This is my story.

This is my song.

Praising my Savior all the day long.

Dillon sings softly as the pallbearers do their thing, but I don't focus on them or how short my time has been with my dad. I focus on the second chance I had with him, and all of the memories we made count.

With all this dancing through my head, I

pull Mona and my son close, knowing how important it is to appreciate the gifts before us and abandon the hurts holding us captive.

ABOUT THE AUTHOR

If T.I. isn't writing a book, she's reading one. She's proud to be a part of a tiny town in South Carolina where she is surrounded by loved ones and country fields.

For a complete list of Lowe's published books, biography, upcoming events, and other information, visit http://www.tilowe.com/ and be sure to check out her blog, COFFEE CUP, while you're there!

She loves to connect with her reading friends.

ti.lowe@yahoo.com
https://www.facebook.com/T.I.Lowe/

Made in the USA
Columbia, SC
14 October 2020